# The
# Story Girl

### L. M. MONTGOMERY

SEAL BOOKS
McClelland-Bantam, Inc.
Toronto

This low-priced Seal Book
has been completely reset in a typeface
designed for easy reading, and was printed
from new plates. It contains the complete
text of the original hardcover edition.
NOT ONE WORD HAS BEEN OMITTED.

THE STORY GIRL

A Seal Book / published by arrangement with
the author's estate

PRINTING HISTORY

First Canadian edition / September 1944
Seal edition / August 1987

ISBN 0-7704-42191-1

PRINTED IN CANADA

COVER PRINTED IN U.S.A.

U      0 9 8 7 6 5 4

# The
# Story Girl

# Contents

# CHAPTER I

# The
# Home of
# Our Fathers

"I DO like a road, because you can be always wondering what is at the end of it."

The Story Girl said that once upon a time. Felix and I, on the May morning when we left Toronto for Prince Edward Island, had not then heard her say it, and, indeed, were but barely aware of the existence of such a person as the Story Girl. We did not know her at all under that name. We knew only that a cousin, Sara Stanley, whose mother, our Aunt Felicity, was dead, was living down on the Island with Uncle Roger and Aunt Olivia King, on a farm adjoining the old King homestead in Carlisle. We supposed we should get acquainted with her when we reached there, and we had an idea, from Aunt Olivia's letters to father, that she would be quite a jolly creature. Further than that we did not think about her. We were more interested in Felicity and Cecily and Dan, who lived on the homestead and would therefore be our roofmates for a season.

But the spirit of the Story Girl's yet unuttered remark was thrilling in our hearts that morning, as the train pulled out of Toronto. We were faring forth on a long road; and, though we had some idea what would be at the end of it, there was enough glamour of the unknown about it to lend a wonderful charm to our speculations concerning it.

We were delighted at the thought of seeing father's old home, and living among the haunts of his boyhood. He had talked so much to us about it, and described its scenes so often and so minutely, that he had inspired us with some of his own deep-seated affection for it—an affection that had never waned in all his years of exile. We had a vague feeling that we, somehow, belonged there, in that cradle of our family, though we had never seen it. We had always looked forward eagerly to the promised day when father would take us "down home," to the old house with the spruces behind it and the famous "King orchard" before it—when we might ramble in "Uncle Stephen's Walk," drink from the deep well with the Chinese roof over it, stand on "the Pulpit Stone," and eat apples from our "birthday trees."

The time had come sooner than we had dared to hope; but father could not take us after all. His firm asked him to go to Rio de Janeiro that spring to take charge of their new branch there. It was too good a chance to lose, for father was a poor man and it meant promotion and increase of salary; but it also meant the temporary breaking up of our home. Our mother had died before either of us was old enough to remember her; father could not take us to Rio de Janeiro. In the end he decided to send us to Uncle Alec and Aunt Janet down on the homestead; and our housekeeper, who belonged to the Island and was now returning to it, took charge of us on the journey. I fear she had an anxious trip of it, poor woman! She was constantly in a quite justifiable terror lest we should be lost or killed; she must have felt great relief when she reached Charlottetown and handed us over to the keeping of Uncle Alec. Indeed, she said as much.

"The fat one isn't so bad. He isn't so quick to move and get out of your sight while you're winking as the thin one. But the only safe way to travel with those young ones would be to have 'em both tied to you with a short rope—a *mighty* short rope."

"The fat one" was Felix, who was very sensitive about his plumpness. He was always taking exercises to make him thin, with the dismal result that he became fatter all the time. He vowed that he didn't care; but he *did* care terribly, and he glowered at Mrs. MacLaren in a most undutiful fashion. He had never liked her since the day she had told him he would soon be as broad as he was long.

For my own part, I was rather sorry to see her going; and she cried over us and wished us well; but we had forgotten all about her by the time we reached the open country, driving along, one on either side of Uncle Alec, whom we loved from the moment we saw him. He was a small man, with thin, delicate features, close-clipped gray beard, and large, tired, blue eyes—father's eyes over again. We knew that Uncle Alec was fond of children and was heart-glad to welcome "Alan's boys." We felt at home with him, and were not afraid to ask him questions on any subject that came uppermost in our minds. We became very good friends with him on that twenty-four-mile drive.

Much to our disappointment it was dark when we reached Carlisle—too dark to see anything very distinctly, as we drove up the lane of the old King homestead on the hill. Behind us a young moon was hanging over southwestern meadows of spring-time peace, but all about us were the soft, moist shadows of a May night. We peered eagerly through the gloom.

"There's the big willow, Bev," whispered Felix excitedly, as we turned in at the gate.

There it was, in truth—the tree Grandfather King had planted when he returned one evening from ploughing in the brook field and stuck the willow switch he had used all day in the soft soil by the gate.

It had taken root and grown; our father and our uncles and aunts had played in its shadow; and now it was a massive thing, with a huge girth of trunk and great spreading boughs, each of them as large as a tree in itself.

"I'm going to climb it to-morrow," I said joyfully.

Off to the right was a dim, branching place which we knew was the orchard; and on our left, among sibilant spruces and firs, was the old, whitewashed house—from which presently a light gleamed through an open door, and Aunt Janet, a big, bustling, sonsy woman, with full-blown peony cheeks, came to welcome us.

Soon after we were at supper in the kitchen, with its low, dark, raftered ceiling from which substantial hams and flitches of bacon were hanging. Everything was just as father had described it. We felt that we had come home, leaving exile behind us.

Felicity, Cecily, and Dan were sitting opposite us, staring at us when they thought we would be too busy eating to see them. We tried to stare at them when *they* were eating; and as a result we were always catching each other at it and feeling cheap and embarrassed.

Dan was the oldest; he was my age—thirteen. He was a lean, freckled fellow with rather long, lank, brown hair and the shapely King nose. We recognized it at once. His mouth was his own, however, for it was like to no mouth on either the King or the Ward side; and nobody would have been anxious to claim it, for it was an undeniably ugly one—long and narrow and twisted. But it could grin in friendly fashion, and both Felix and I felt that we were going to like Dan.

Felicity was twelve. She had been called after Aunt Felicity, who was the twin sister of Uncle Felix. Aunt Felicity and Uncle Felix, as father had often told us, had died on the same day, far apart, and were buried side by side in the old Carlisle graveyard.

We had known, from Aunt Olivia's letters, that Felicity was the beauty of the connection, and we had been curious to see her on that account. She fully justified our expectations. She was plump and dimpled, with big, dark-blue, heavy-lidded eyes, soft, feathery, golden curls, and a pink and white skin—"the King complexion." The Kings were noted for their noses and complexion. Felicity had also delightful hands and wrists. At every turn of them a dimple showed itself. It was a pleasure to wonder what her elbows must be like.

She was very nicely dressed in a pink print and a frilled muslin apron; and we understood, from something Dan said, that she had "dressed up" in honour of our coming. This made us feel quite important. So far as we knew, no feminine creatures had ever gone to the pains of dressing up on our account before.

Cecily, who was eleven, was pretty also—or would have been had Felicity not been there. Felicity rather took the colour from other girls. Cecily looked pale and thin beside her; but she had dainty little features, smooth brown hair of satin sheen, and mild brown eyes, with just a hint of demureness in them now and again. We remembered that Aunt Olivia had written to father that Cecily was a true Ward—she had no sense of humour. We did not know what this meant, but we thought it was not exactly complimentary.

Still, we were both inclined to think we would like Cecily better than Felicity. To be sure, Felicity was a stunning beauty. But, with the swift and unerring intuition of childhood, which feels in a moment what it sometimes takes maturity much time to perceive, we realized that she was rather too well aware of her good looks. In brief, we saw that Felicity was vain.

"It's a wonder the Story Girl isn't over to see you," said Uncle Alec. "She's been quite wild with excitement about your coming."

"She hasn't been very well all day," explained Cecily, "and Aunt Olivia wouldn't let her come out in the night air. She made her go to bed instead. The Story Girl was awfully disappointed."

"Who is the Story Girl?" asked Felix.

"Oh, Sara—Sara Stanley. We call her the Story Girl partly because she's such a hand to tell stories—oh, I can't begin to describe it—and partly because Sara Ray, who lives at the foot of the hill, often comes up to play with us, and it is awkward to have two girls of the same name in the same crowd. Besides, Sara Stanley doesn't like her name and she'd rather be called the Story Girl."

Dan, speaking for the first time, rather sheepishly volunteered the information that Peter had also been intending to come over but had to go home to take some flour to his mother instead.

"Peter?" I questioned. I had never heard of any Peter.

"He is your Uncle Roger's handy boy," said Uncle Alec. "His name is Peter Craig, and he is a real smart little chap. But he's got his share of mischief, that same lad."

"He wants to be Felicity's beau," said Dan slyly.

"Don't talk silly nonsense, Dan," said Aunt Janet severely.

Felicity toosed her golden head and shot an unsisterly glance at Dan.

"I wouldn't be very likely to have a hired boy for a beau," she observed.

We saw that her anger was real, not affected. Evidently Peter was not an admirer of whom Felicity was proud.

We were very hungry boys; and when we had eaten all we could—and oh, what suppers Aunt Janet always spread!—we discovered that we were very tired also—too tired to go out and explore our ancestral domains, as we would have liked to do, despite the dark.

We were quite willing to go to bed; and presently we found ourselves tucked away upstairs in the very room, looking out eastward into the spruce grove, which father had once occupied. Dan shared it with us, sleeping in a bed of his own in the opposite corner. The sheets and pillow-slips were fragrant with lavender, and one of Grandmother King's noted patchwork quilts was over us. The window was open and we heard the frogs singing down in the swamp of the brook meadow. We had heard frogs sing in Ontario, of course; but certainly Prince Edward Island frogs were more tuneful and mellow. Or was it simply the glamour of old family traditions and tales which was over us, lending its magic to all sights and sounds around us? This was home—father's home—*our* home! We had never lived long enough in any one house to develop a feeling of affection for it; but here, under the roof-tree built by Grand-Grandfather King ninety years ago, that feeling swept into our boyish hearts and souls like a flood of living sweetness and tenderness.

"Just think, those are the very frogs father listened to when he was a little boy," whispered Felix.

"They can hardly be the *same* frogs," I objected doubtfully, not feeling very certain about the possible longevity of frogs. "It's twenty years since father left home."

"Well, they're the descendants of the frogs he heard," said Felix, "and they're singing in the same swamp. That's near enough."

Our door was open and in their room across the narrow hall the girls were preparing for bed, and talking rather more loudly than they might have done had they realized how far their sweet, shrill voices carried.

"What do you think of the boys?" asked Cecily.

"Beverley is handsome, but Felix is too fat," answered Felicity promptly.

Felix twitched the quilt rather viciously and grunted. But I began to think I would like Felicity. It might not be altogether her fault that she was vain. How could she help it when she looked in the mirror?

"I think they're both nice and nice looking," said Cecily.

Dear little soul!

"I wonder what the Story Girl will think of them," said Felicity, as if, after all, that was the main thing.

Somehow, we, too, felt that it was. We felt that if the Story Girl did not approve of us it made little difference who else did or did not.

"I wonder if the Story Girl is pretty," said Felix aloud.

"No, she isn't," said Dan instantly, from across the room. "But you'll think she is while she's talking to you. Everybody does. It's only when you go away from her that you find out she isn't a bit pretty after all."

The girls' door shut with a bang. Silence fell over the house. We drifted into the land of sleep, wondering if the Story Girl would like us.

# CHAPTER II

# A Queen of Hearts

I WAKENED shortly after sunrise. The pale May sunshine was showering through the spruces, and a chill, inspiring wind was tossing the boughs about.

"Felix, wake up," I whispered, shaking him.

"What's the matter?" he murmured reluctantly.

"It's morning. Let's get up and go down and out. I can't wait another minute to see the places father has told us of."

We slipped out of bed and dressed, without arousing Dan, who was still slumbering soundly, his mouth wide open, and his bed-clothes kicked off on the floor. I had hard work to keep Felix from trying to see if he could "shy" a marble into that tempting open mouth. I told him it would waken Dan, who would then likely insist on getting up and accompanying us, and it would be so much nicer to go by ourselves for the first time.

Everything was very still as we crept downstairs. Out in the kitchen we heard some one, presumably Uncle Alec, lighting the fire; but the heart of the house had not yet begun to beat for the day.

We paused a moment in the hall to look at the big "Grandfather" clock. It was not going, but it seemed like an old, familiar acquaintance to us, with the gilt balls on its three peaks; the little dial and pointer which would indicate the changes of the moon, and the very dent in its wooden door which father had made when he was a boy, by kicking it in a fit of naughtiness.

Then we opened the front door and stepped out, rapture swelling in our bosoms. There was a rare breeze from the south blowing to meet us; the shadows of the spruces were long and clear-cut; the exquisite skies of early morning, blue and wind-winnowed, were over us; away to the west, beyond the brook field, was a long valley and a hill purple with firs and laced with still leafless beeches and maples.

Behind the house was a grove of fir and spruce, a dim, cool place where the winds were fond of purring and where there was always a resinous, woodsy odour. On the further side of it was a thick plantation of slender silver birches and whispering poplars; and beyond it was Uncle Roger's house.

Right before us, girt about with its trim spruce hedge, was the famous King orchard, the history of which was woven into our earliest recollections. We knew all about it, from father's descriptions, and in fancy we had roamed in it many a time and oft.

It was now nearly sixty years since it had had its beginning, when Grandfather King brought his bride home. Before the wedding he had fenced off the big south meadow that sloped to the sun; it was the finest, most fertile field on the farm, and the neighbours told young Abraham King that he would raise many a fine crop of wheat in that meadow. Abraham King smiled and, being a man of few words, said nothing; but in his mind he had a vision of the years to be, and in that vision he saw, not rippling acres of harvest gold, but great, leafy avenues of wide-spreading trees laden with fruit to gladden the eyes of children and grandchildren yet unborn.

It was a vision to develop slowly into fulfilment. Grandfather King was in no hurry. He did not set his whole orchard out at once, for he wished it to grow with his life and history, and be bound up with all of good and joy that should come to his household. So the morning after he had brought his young wife home they went together to the south meadow and planted their bridal trees. These trees were no longer living; but they had been when father was a boy, and every spring bedecked themselves in blossom as delicately tinted as Elizabeth King's face when she walked through the old south meadow in the morn of her life and love.

When a son was born to Abraham and Elizabeth a tree was planted in the orchard for him. They had fourteen children in all, and each child had its "birth tree." Every family festival was commemorated in like fashion, and every beloved visitor who spent a night under their roof was expected to plant a tree in the orchard. So it came to pass that every tree in it was a fair green monument to some love or delight of the vanished years. And each grandchild had its tree, there, also, set out by grandfather when the tidings of its birth reached him; not always an apple tree—perhaps it was a plum, or cherry or pear. But it was always known by the name of the person for whom, or by whom, it was planted; and Felix and I knew as much about "Aunt Felicity's pears," and "Aunt Julia's cherries," and "Uncle Alec's apples," and the "Rev. Mr. Scott's plums," as if we had been born and bred among them.

And now we had come to the orchard; it was before us; we had only to open that little whitewashed gate in the hedge and we might find ourselves in its storied domain. But before we reached the gate we glanced to our left, along the grassy, spruce-bordered lane which led over to Uncle Roger's; and at the entrance of that lane we saw a girl standing, with a gray cat at her feet. She lifted her hand and beckoned blithely to us; and, the orchard forgotten, we followed her summons. For we knew that this must be the Story Girl; and in that gay and graceful gesture was an allurement not to be gainsaid or denied.

We looked at her as we drew near with such interest that we forgot to feel shy. No, she was not pretty. She was tall for her fourteen years, slim and straight; around her long, white face—rather too long and too white—fell sleek, dark-brown curls, tied above either ear with rosettes of scarlet ribbon. Her large curving mouth was as red as a poppy, and she had brilliant, almond-shaped, hazel eyes; but we did not think her pretty.

Then she spoke; she said,

"Good morning."

Never had we heard a voice like hers. Never, in all my life since, have I heard such a voice. I cannot describe it. I might say it was clear; I might say it was sweet; I might say it was vibrant and far-reaching and bell-like; all this would be true, but it would give you no real idea of the peculiar quality which made the Story Girl's voice what it was.

If voices had colour, hers would have been like a rainbow. It made words *live*. Whatever she said became a breathing entity, not a mere verbal statement or utterance. Felix and I were too young to understand or analyze the impression it made upon us; but we instantly felt at her greeting that it *was* a good morning—a surpassingly good morning—the very best morning that had ever happened in this most excellent of worlds.

"You are Felix and Beverley," she went on, shaking our

hands with an air of frank comradeship, which was very different
from the shy, feminine advances of Felicity and Cecily. From that
moment we were as good friends as if we had known each other
for a hundred years. "I am glad to see you. I was so disappointed
I couldn't go over last night. I got up early this morning,
though, for I felt sure you would be up early, too, and that
you'd like to have me tell you about things. I can tell things so
much better than Felicity or Cecily. Do you think Felicity is *very*
pretty?"

"She's the prettiest girl I ever saw," I said enthusiastically,
remembering that Felicity had called me handsome.

"The boys all think so," said the Story Girl, not, I fancied,
quite well pleased. "And I suppose she is. She is a splendid
cook, too, though she is only twelve. *I* can't cook. I am trying
to learn, but I don't make much progress. Aunt Olivia says I
haven't enough natural gumption ever to be a cook; but I'd love
to be able to make as good cakes and pies as Felicity can make.
But then, Felicity is stupid. It's not ill-natured of me to say
that. It's just the truth, and you'd soon find it out for your-
selves. I like Felicity very well, but she *is* stupid. Cecily is ever
so much cleverer. Cecily's a dear. So is Uncle Alec; and Aunt
Janet is pretty nice, too."

"What is Aunt Olivia like?" asked Felix.

"Aunt Olivia is very pretty. She is just like a pansy—all
velvety and purply and goldy."

Felix and I *saw*, somewhere inside of our heads, a velvet and
purple and gold pansy-woman, just as the Story Girl spoke.

"But is she *nice*?" I asked. That was the main question about
grown-ups. Their looks mattered little to us.

"She is lovely. But she is twenty-nine, you know. That's
pretty old. She doesn't bother me much. Aunt Janet says that I'd
have no bringing up at all, if it wasn't for her. Aunt Olivia says
children should just be let *come* up—that everything else is
settled for them long before they are born. I don't understand
that. Do you?"

No, we did not. But it was our experience that grown-ups
had a habit of saying things hard to understand.

"What is Uncle Roger like?" was our next question.

"Well, *I* like Uncle Roger," said the Story Girl meditatively.
"He is big and jolly. But he teases people too much. You ask
him a serious question and you get a ridiculous answer. He

hardly ever scolds or gets cross, though, and *that* is something. He is an old bachelor."

"Doesn't he ever mean to get married?" asked Felix.

"I don't know. Aunt Olivia wishes he would, because she's tired keeping house for him, and she wants to go to Aunt Julia in California. But she says he'll never get married, because he is looking for perfection, and when he finds her she won't have *him*."

By this time we were all sitting down on the gnarled roots of the spruces, and the big gray cat came over and made friends with us. He was a lordly animal, with a silver-gray coat beautifully marked with darker stripes. With such colouring most cats would have had white or silver feet; but he had four black paws and a black nose. Such points gave him an air of distinction, and marked him out as quite different from the common or garden variety of cats. He seemed to be a cat with a tolerably good opinion of himself, and his response to our advances was slightly tinged with condescension.

"This isn't Topsy, is it?" I asked. I knew at once that the question was a foolish one. Topsy, the cat of which father had talked, had flourished thirty years before, and all her nine lives could scarcely have lasted so long.

"No, but it is Topsy's great-great-great-great-grandson," said the Story Girl gravely. "His name is Paddy and he is my own particular cat. We have barn cats, but Paddy never associates with them. I am very good friends with all cats. They are so sleek and comfortable and dignified. And it is so easy to make them happy. Oh, I'm so glad you boys have come to live here. Nothing ever happens here, except days, so we have to make our own good times. We were short of boys before—only Dan and Peter to four girls."

"*Four* girls? Oh, yes, Sara Ray. Felicity mentioned her. What is she like? Where does she live?"

"Just down the hill. You can't see the house for the spruce bush. Sara is a nice girl. She's only eleven, and her mother is dreadfully strict. She never allows Sara to read a single story. *Just* you fancy! Sara's conscience is always troubling her for doing things she's sure her mother won't approve, but it never prevents her from doing them. It only spoils her fun. Uncle Roger says that a mother who won't let you do anything, and a conscience that won't let you enjoy anything is an awful combination, and he doesn't wonder Sara is pale and thin and nervous. But, between you and me, I believe the real reason is that her mother doesn't give her half enough to eat. Not that she's mean, you know—but she thinks it isn't healthy for children to eat much, or anything but certain things. Isn't it fortunate we weren't born into that sort of a family?"

"I think it's awful lucky we were all born into the same family," Felix remarked.

"Isn't it? I've often thought so. And I've often thought what a dreadful thing it would have been if Grandfather and Grandmother King had never got married to each other. I don't suppose there would have been a single one of us children here at all; or if we were, we would be part somebody else and that would be almost as bad. When I think it all over I can't feel too thankful that Grandfather and Grandmother King happened to marry each other, when there were so many other people they might have married."

Felix and I shivered. We felt suddenly that we had escaped a dreadful danger—the danger of having been born somebody else. But it took the Story Girl to make us realize just how dreadful it was and what a terrible risk we had run years before we, or our parents either, had existed.

"Who lives over there?" I asked, pointing to a house across the fields.

"Oh, that belongs to the Awkward Man. His name is Jasper Dale, but everybody calls him the Awkward Man. And they do say he writes poetry. He calls his place Golden Milestone. I know why, because I've read Longfellow's poems. He never goes into society because he is so awkward. The girls laugh at him and he doesn't like it. I know a story about him and I'll tell it to you sometime."

"And who lives in that other house?" asked Felix, looking over the westering valley where a little gray roof was visible among the trees.

"Old Peg Bowen. She's very queer. She lives there with a lot of pet animals in winter, and in summer she roams over the country and begs her meals. They say she is crazy. People have always tried to frighten us children into good behaviour by telling us that Peg Bowen would catch us if we didn't behave. I'm not so frightened of her as I once was, but I don't think I would like to be caught by her. Sara Ray is dreadfully scared of her. Peter

Craig says she is a witch and that he bets she's at the bottom of it when the butter won't come. But I don't believe *that*. Witches are so scarce nowadays. There may be some somewhere in the world, but it's not likely there are any here right in Prince Edward Island. They used to be very plenty long ago. I know some splendid witch stories I'll tell you some day. They'll just make your blood freeze in your veins."

We hadn't a doubt of it. If anybody could freeze the blood in our veins this girl with the wonderful voice could. But it was a May morning, and our young blood was running blithely in our veins. We suggested that a visit to the orchard would be more agreeable.

"All right. I know stories about it, too," she said, as we walked across the yard, followed by Paddy of the waving tail. "Oh, aren't you glad it is spring? The beauty of winter is that it makes you appreciate spring."

The latch of the gate clicked under the Story Girl's hand, and the next moment we were in the King orchard.

# CHAPTER III

# *Legends of the Old Orchard*

OUTSIDE of the orchard the grass was only beginning to grow green; but here, sheltered by the spruce hedges from uncertain winds and sloping to southern suns, it was already like a wonderful velvet carpet; the leaves on the trees were beginning to come out in woolly, grayish clusters; and there were purple-pencilled white violets at the base of the Pulpit Stone.

"It's all just as father described it," said Felix with a blissful sigh, "and there's the well with the Chinese roof."

We hurried over to it, treading on the spears of mint that were beginning to shoot up about it. It was a very deep well, and the curb was of rough, undressed stones. Over it, the queer, pagoda-like roof, built by Uncle Stephen on his return from a voyage to China, was covered with yet leafless vines.

"It's so pretty when the vines leaf out and hang down in long festoons," said the Story Girl. "The birds build their nests in it. A pair of wild canaries come here every summer. And ferns grow out between the stones of the well as far down as you can see. The water is lovely. Uncle Edward preached his finest sermon about the Bethlehem well where David's soldiers went to get him water, and he illustrated it by describing his old well at the homestead—this very well—and how in foreign lands he had longed for its sparkling water. So you see it is quite famous."

"There's a cup just like the one that used to be here in father's time," exclaimed Felix, pointing to an old-fashioned shallow cup of clouded blue ware on a little shelf inside the curb.

"It is the very same cup," said the Story Girl impressively. "Isn't it an amazing thing? That cup has been here for forty years, and hundreds of people have drunk from it, and it has never been broken. Aunt Julia dropped it down the well once, but they fished it up, not hurt a bit except for that little nick in the rim. *I* think it is bound up with the fortunes of the King family, like the Luck of Edenhall in Longfellow's poem. It is the last cup of Grandmother's King's second best set. Her best set is still complete. Anut Olivia has it. You must get her to show it to you. It's so pretty, with red berries all over it, and the funniest little pot-bellied cream jug. Aunt Olivia never uses it except on a family anniversary."

We took a drink from the blue cup and then went to find our birthday trees. We were rather disappointed to find them quite large, sturdy ones. It seemed to us that they should still be in the sapling stage corresponding to our boyhood.

"Your apples are lovely to eat," the Story Girl said to me, "but Felix's are only good for pies. Those two big trees behind them are the twins' trees—my mother and Uncle Felix, you know. The apples are so dead sweet that nobody but us children and the French boys can eat them. And that tall, slender tree over there, with the branches all growing straight up, is a seedling that came up of itself, and *nobody* can eat its apples, they are so sour and bitter. Even the pigs won't eat them. Aunt Janet tried to make pies of them once, because she said she hated to see them going to waste. But she never tried again. She said it was better to waste apples alone than apples and sugar too. And then she tried giving them away to the French hired men, but they wouldn't even carry them home."

The Story Girl's words fell on the morning air like pearls and diamonds. Even her prepositions and conjunctions had untold charm, hinting at mystery and laughter and magic bound up in everything she mentioned. Apple pies and sour seedlings and pigs became straightway invested with a glamour of romance.

"I like to hear you talk," said Felix in his grave, stodgy way.

"Everybody does," said the Story Girl coolly. "I'm glad you like the way I talk. But I want you to like *me*, too—*as well as* you like Felicity and Cecily. Not *better.* I wanted that once but I've got over it. I found out in Sunday School, the day the minister taught our class, that it was selfish. But I want you to like me *as well.*"

"Well, *I* will, for one," said Felix emphatically. I think he was remembering that Felicity had called him fat.

Cecily now joined us. It appeared that it was Felicity's morning to help prepare breakfast, therefore she could not come. We all went to Uncle Stephen's Walk.

This was a double row of apple trees, running down the western side of the orchard. Uncle Stephen was the first born of Abraham and Elizabeth King. He had none of grandfather's abiding love for woods and meadows and the kindly ways of the warm red earth. Grandmother King had been a Ward, and in Uncle Stephen the blood of that seafaring race claimed its own. To sea he must go, despite the pleadings and tears of a reluctant mother; and it was from the sea he came to set out his avenue in the orchard with trees brought from a foreign land.

Then he sailed away again—and the ship was never heard of more. The gray first came in grandmother's brown hair in those months of waiting. Then, for the first time, the orchard heard the sound of weeping and was consecrated by a sorrow.

"When the blossoms come out it's wonderful to walk here," said the Story Girl. "It's like a dream of fairyland—as if you were walking in a king's palace. The apples are delicious, and in winter it's a splendid place for coasting."

From the Walk we went to the Pulpit Stone—a huge gray boulder, as high as a man's head, in the southeastern corner. It was straight and smooth in front, but sloped down in natural steps behind, with a ledge midway on which one could stand. It had played an important part in the games of our uncles and aunts, being fortified castle, Indian ambush, throne, pulpit, or concert platform, as occasion required. Uncle Edward had preached his first sermon at the age of eight from that old gray boulder; and Aunt Julia, whose voice was to delight thousands, sang her earliest madrigals there.

The Story Girl mounted to the ledge, sat on the rim, and looked at us. Pat sat gravely at its base and daintily washed his face with his black paws.

"Now for your stories about the orchard," said I.

"There are two important ones," said the Story Girl. "The story of the Poet Who Was Kissed, and the Tale of the Family Ghost. Which one shall I tell?"

"Tell them both," said Felix greedily, "but tell the ghost one first."

"I don't know." The Story Girl looked dubious. "That sort of story ought to be told in the twilight among the shadows. Then it would frighten the souls out of your bodies."

We thought it might be more agreeable not to have the souls frightened out of our bodies, and we voted for the Family Ghost.

"Ghost stories are more comfortable in daytime," said Felix.

The Story Girl began it and we listened avidly. Cecily, who had heard it many times before, listened just as eagerly as we did. She declared to me afterwards that no matter how often the Story Girl told a story it always seemed as new and exciting as if you had just heard it for the first time.

"Long, long ago," began the Story Girl, her voice giving us an impression of remote antiquity, "even before Grandfather King was born, an orphan cousin of his lived here with his parents. Her name was Emily King. She was very small and very sweet. She had soft brown eyes that were too timid to look straight at anybody—like Cecily's there—and long, sleek, brown curls—like mine; and she had a tiny birthmark like a pink butterfly on one cheek—right here.

"Of course, there was no orchard here then. It was just a field; but there was a clump of white birches in it, right where that big, spreading tree of Uncle Alec's is now, and Emily liked to sit among the ferns under the birches and read or sew. She had a lover. His name was Malcolm Ward and he was as handsome as a prince. She loved him with all her heart and he loved her the same; but they had never spoken about it. They used to meet under the birches and talk about everything except love. One day he told her he was coming the next day to ask *a very important question*, and he wanted to find her under the birches when he came. Emily promised to meet him there. I am sure she stayed awake that night, thinking about it, and wondering what the important question would be, although she knew perfectly well. *I* would have. And the next day she dressed herself beautifully in her best pale blue muslin and sleeked her curls and went smiling to the birches. And while she was waiting there, thinking such lovely thoughts, a neighbour's boy came running up—a boy who didn't know about her romance—and cried out that Malcolm Ward had been killed by his gun going off accidentally. Emily just put her hands to her heart—so—and fell, all white and broken among the ferns. And when she came back to life she never cried or lamented. She was *changed*. She was never, never like herself again; and she was never contented unless she was dressed in her blue muslin and waiting under the birches. She got paler and paler every day, but the pink butterfly grew redder, until it looked just like a stain of blood on her white cheek. When the winter came she died. But next spring"—the Story Girl dropped her voice to a whisper that was as audible and thrilling as her louder tones—"people began to tell that Emily was sometimes seen waiting under the birches still. Nobody knew just who told it first. But more than one person saw her. Grandfather saw her when he was a little boy. And my mother saw her once."

"Did *you* ever see her?" asked Felix skeptically.

"No, but I shall some day, if I keep on believing in her," said the Story Girl confidently.

"*I* wouldn't like to see her. I'd be afraid," said Cecily with a shiver.

"There wouldn't be anything to be afraid of," said the Story Girl reassuringly. "It's not as if it were a strange ghost. It's our own family ghost, so of course it wouldn't hurt us."

We were not so sure of this. Ghosts were unchancy folk, even if they were our family ghosts. The Story Girl had made the tale very real to us. We were glad we had not heard it in the evening. How could we ever have got back to the house through the shadows and swaying branches of a darkening orchard? As it was, we were almost afraid to look up it, lest we should see the waiting, blue-clad Emily under Uncle Alec's tree. But all we saw was Felicity, tearing over the green sward, her curls streaming behind her in a golden cloud.

"Felicity's afraid she has missed something," remarked the Story Girl in a tone of quiet amusement. "Is your breakfast ready, Felicity, or have I time to tell the boys the Story of the Poet Who Was Kissed?"

"Breakfast is ready, but we can't have it till father is through attending to the sick cow, so you will likely have time," answered Felicity.

Felix and I couldn't keep our eyes off her. Crimson-cheeked, shining-eyed from her haste, her face was like a rose of youth. But when the Story Girl spoke, we forgot to look at Felicity.

"About ten years after Grandfather and Grandmother King were married, a young man came to visit them. He was a

distant relative of grandmother's and he was a Poet. He was just
beginning to be famous. He was *very* famous afterward. He came
into the orchard to write a poem, and he fell asleep with his
head on a bench that used to be under grandfather's tree. Then
Great-Aunt Edith came into the orchard. She was not a Great-
Aunt then, of course. She was only eighteen, with red lips and
black, black hair and eyes. They say she was always full of
mischief. She had been away and had just come home, and she
didn't know about the Poet. But when she saw him, sleeping
there, she thought he was a cousin they had been expecting from
Scotland. And she tiptoed up—so—and bent over—so—and
kissed his cheek. Then he opened his big blue eyes and looked
up into Edith's face. She blushed as red as a rose, for she knew
she had done a dreadful thing. This could not be her cousin
from Scotland. She knew, for he had written so to her, that he
had eyes as black as her own. Edith ran away and hid; and of
course she felt still worse when she found out that he was a
famous poet. But he wrote one of his most beautiful poems on it
afterwards and sent it to her—and it was published in one of his
books."

We had *seen* it all—the sleeping genius—the roguish, red-
lipped girl—the kiss dropped as lightly as a rose-petal on the
sunburned cheek.

"They should have got married," said Felix.

"Well, in a book they would have, but you see this was in
real life," said the Story Girl. "We sometimes act the story out.
I like it when Peter plays the poet. I don't like it when Dan is
the poet because he is so freckled and screws his eyes up so
tight. But you can hardly ever coax Peter to be the poet—except
when Felicity is Edith—and Dan is so obliging that way."

"What is Peter like?" I asked.

"Peter is splendid. His mother lives on the Markdale road
and washes for a living. Peter's father ran away and left them
when Peter was only three years old. He has never come back,
and they don't know whether he is alive or dead. Isn't that a nice
way to behave to your family? Peter has worked for his board
ever since he was six. Uncle Roger sends him to school, and pays
him wages in summer. We all like Peter, except Felicity."

"I like Peter well enough in his place," said Felicity primly,
"but you make far too much of him, mother says. He is only a
hired boy, and he hasn't been well brought up, and hasn't much

education. *I* don't think you should make such an equal of him as you do."

Laughter rippled over the Story Girl's face as shadow waves go over ripe wheat before a wind.

"Peter is a real gentleman, and he is more interesting than *you* could ever be, if you were brought up and educated for a hundred years," she said.

"He can hardly write," said Felicity.

"William the Conqueror couldn't write at all," said the Story Girl crushingly.

"He never goes to church, and he never says his prayers," retorted Felicity, uncrushed.

"I do, too," said Peter himself, suddenly appearing through a little gap in the hedge. "I say my prayers sometimes."

This Peter was a slim, shapely fellow, with laughing black eyes and thick black curls. Early in the season as it was, he was barefooted. His attire consisted of a faded, gingham shirt and a scanty pair of corduroy knickerbockers; but he wore it with such an unconscious air of purple and fine linen that he seemed to be much better dressed than he really was.

"You don't pray very often," insisted Felicity.

"Well, God will be all the more likely to listen to me if I don't pester Him all the time," argued Peter.

This was rank heresy to Felicity, but the Story Girl looked as if she thought there might be something in it.

"You *never* go to church, anyhow," continued Felicity, determined not to be argued down.

"Well, I ain't going to church till I've made up my mind whether I'm going to be a Methodist or a Presbyterian. Aunt Jane was a Methodist. My mother ain't much of anything but *I* mean to be something. It's more respectable to be a Methodist or a Presbyterian, or *something*, than not to be anything. When I've settled what I'm to be I'm going to church same as you."

"That's not the same as being *born* something," said Felicity loftily.

"I think it's a good deal better to pick your own religion than have to take it just because it was what your folks had," retorted Peter.

"Now, never mind quarrelling," said Cecily. "You leave Peter alone, Felicity. Peter, this is Beverley King, and this is Felix. And we're all going to be good friends and have a lovely

summer together. Think of the games we can have! But if you
go squabbling you'll spoil it all. Peter, what are you going to do
to-day?"

"Harrow the wood field and dig your Aunt Olivia's flower
beds."

"Aunt Olivia and I planted the sweet peas yesterday," said
the Story Girl, "and I planted a little bed of my own. I am *not*
going to dig them up this year to see if they have sprouted. It is
bad for them. I shall try to cultivate patience, no matter how
long they are coming up."

"I am going to help mother plant the vegetable garden
to-day," said Felicity.

"Oh, I never like the vegetable garden," said the Story Girl.
"Except when I am hungry. Then I *do* like to go and look at the
nice little rows of onions and beets. But I love a flower garden. I
think I could be always good if I lived in a garden all the time."

"Adam and Eve lived in a garden all the time," said Felicity,
"and *they* were far from being always good."

"They mightn't have kept good as long as they did if they
hadn't lived in a garden," said the Story Girl.

We were now summoned to breakfast. Peter and the Story
Girl slipped away through the gap, followed by Paddy, and the
rest of us walked up the orchard to the house.

"Well, what do you think of the Story Girl?" asked Felicity.

"She's just fine," said Felix, enthusiastically. "I never heard
anything like her to tell stories."

"She can't cook," said Felicity, "and she hasn't a good
complexion. Mind you, she says she's going to be an actress
when she grows up. Isn't that dreadful?"

We didn't exactly see why.

"Oh, because actresses are always wicked people," said
Felicity in a shocked tone. "But I daresay the Story Girl will go
and be one just as soon as she can. Her father will back her up
in it. He is an artist, you know."

Evidently Felicity thought artists and actresses and all such
poor trash were members one of another.

"Aunt Olivia says the Story Girl is fascinating," said Cecily.

The very adjective! Felix and I recognized its beautiful
fitness at once. Yes, the Story Girl *was* fascinating and that was
the final word to be said on the subject.

Dan did not come down until breakfast was half over, and

Aunt Janet talked to him after a fashion which made us realize that it would be well to keep, as the piquant country phrase went, from the rough side of her tongue. But all things considered, we liked the prospect of our summer very much. Felicity to look at—the Story Girl to tell us tales of wonder—Cecily to admire us—Dan and Peter to play with—what more could reasonable fellows want?

# CHAPTER IV

# The Wedding Veil of the Proud Princess

WHEN we had lived for a fortnight in Carlisle we belonged there, and the freedom of all its small fry was conferred on us. With Peter and Dan, with Felicity and Cecily and the Story Girl, with pale, gray-eyed little Sara Ray, we were boon companions. We went to school, of course; and certain home chores were assigned to each of us for the faithful performance of which we were held responsible. But we had long hours for play. Even Peter had plenty of spare time when the planting was over.

We got along very well with each other in the main, in spite of some minor differences of opinion. As for the grown-up denizens of our small world, they suited us also.

We adored Aunt Olivia; she was pretty and merry and kind; and, above all, she had mastered to perfection the rare art of letting children alone. If we kept ourselves tolerably clean, and refrained from quarrelling or talking slang, Aunt Olivia did not worry us. Aunt Janet, on the contrary, gave us so much good advice and was so constantly telling us to do this or not to do the other thing, that we could not remember half her instructions, and did not try.

Uncle Roger was, as we had been informed, quite jolly and fond of teasing. We liked him; but we had an uncomfortable feeling that the meaning of his remarks was not always that which met the ear. Sometimes we believed Uncle Roger was making fun of us, and the deadly seriousness of youth in us resented that.

To Uncle Alec we gave our warmest love. We felt that we

always had a friend at court in Uncle Alec, no matter what we did or left undone. And we never had to turn *his* speeches inside out to discover their meaning.

The social life of juvenile Carlisle centred in the day and Sunday Schools. We were especially interested in our Sunday School, for we were fortunate enough to be assigned to a teacher who made our lessons so interesting that we no longer regarded Sunday School attendance as a disagreeable weekly duty; but instead looked forward to it with pleasure, and tried to carry out our teacher's gentle precepts—at least on Mondays and Tuesdays. I am afraid the remembrance grew a little dim the rest of the week.

She was also deeply interested in missions; and one talk on this subject inspired the Story Girl with a desire to do a little home missionary work on her own account. The only thing she could think of, along this line, was to persuade Peter to go to church.

Felicity did not approve of the design, and said so plainly.

"He won't know how to behave, for he's never been inside a church door in his life," she warned the Story Girl. "He'll likely do something awful, and then you'll feel ashamed and wish you'd never asked him to go, and we'll all be disgraced. It's all right to have our mite boxes for the heathen, and send missionaries to them. They're far away and we don't have to associate with them. But *I* don't want to have to sit in a pew with a hired boy."

But the Story Girl undauntedly continued to coax the reluctant Peter. It was not an easy matter. Peter did not come of a churchgoing stock; and besides, he alleged, he had not yet made up his mind whether to be a Presbyterian or a Methodist.

"It isn't a bit of difference which you are," pleaded the Story Girl. "They both go to heaven."

"But one way must be easier or better than the other, or else they'd all be one kind," argued Peter. "I want to find the easiest way. And I've got a hankering after the Methodists. My Aunt Jane was a Methodist."

"Isn't she one still?" asked Felicity pertly.

"Well, I don't know exactly. She's dead," said Peter rebukingly. "Do people go on being just the same after they're dead?"

"No, of course not. They're angels then—not Methodists or anything, but just angels. That is, if they go to heaven."

"S'posen they went to the other place?"

But Felicity's theology broke down at this point. She turned her back on Peter and walked disdainfully away.

The Story Girl returned to the main point with a new argument.

"We have such a lovely minister, Peter. He looked just like the picture of St. John father sent me, only he is old and his hair is white. I know you'd like him. And even if you are going to be a Methodist it won't hurt you to go to the Presbyterian church. The nearest Methodist church is six miles away, at Markdale, and you can't attend there just now. Go to the Presbyterian church until you're old enough to have a horse."

"But s'posen I got too fond of being Presbyterian and couldn't change if I wanted to?" objected Peter.

Altogether, the Story Girl had a hard time of it; but she persevered; and one day she came to us with the announcement that Peter had yielded.

"He's going to church with us to-morrow," she said triumphantly.

We were out in Uncle Roger's hill pasture, sitting on some smooth, round stones under a clump of birches. Behind us was an old gray fence, with violets and dandelions thick in its corners. Below us was the Carlisle valley, with its orchard-embowered homesteads, and fertile meadows. Its upper end was dim with a delicate spring mist. Winds blew up the field like wave upon wave of sweet savour—spice of bracken and balsam.

We were eating little jam "turnovers," which Felicity had made for us. Felicity's turnovers were perfection. I looked at her and wondered why it was not enough that she should be so pretty and capable of making such turnovers. If she were only more interesting! Felicity had not a particle of the nameless charm and allurement which hung about every motion of the Story Girl, and made itself manifest in her lightest word and most careless glance. Ah well, one cannot have every good gift! The Story Girl had no dimples at her slim, brown wrists.

We all enjoyed our turnovers except Sara Ray. She ate hers but she knew she should not have done so. Her mother did not approve of snacks between meals, or of jam turnovers at any time. Once, when Sara was in a brown study, I asked her what she was thinking of.

"I'm trying to think of something ma hasn't forbid," she answered with a sigh.

We were all glad to hear that Peter was going to church, except Felicity. She was full of gloomy forebodings and warnings.

"I'm surprised at you, Felicity King," said Cecily severely. "You ought to be glad that poor boy is going to get started in the right way."

"There's a great big patch on his best pair of trousers," protested Felicity.

"Well, that's better than a hole," said the Story Girl, addressing herself daintily to her turnover. "God won't notice the patch."

"No, but the Carlisle people will," retorted Felicity, in a tone which implied that what the Carlisle people thought was far more important. "And I don't believe that Peter has got a decent stocking to his name. What will you feel like if he goes to church with the skin of his legs showing through the holes, Miss Story Girl?"

"I'm not a bit afraid," said the Story Girl staunchly. "Peter knows better than that."

"Well, all I hope is that he'll wash behind his ears," said Felicity resignedly.

"How is Pat to-day?" asked Cecily, by way of changing the conversation.

"Pat isn't a bit better. He just mopes about the kitchen," said the Story Girl anxiously. "I went out to the barn and I saw a mouse. I had a stick in my hand and I fetched a swipe at it—so. I killed it stone dead. Then I took it in to Paddy. Will you believe it? He wouldn't even look at it. I'm so worried. Uncle Roger says he needs a dose of physic. But how is he to be made take it, that's the question. I mixed a powder in some milk and tried to pour it down his throat while Peter held him. Just look at the scratches I got! And the milk went everywhere except down Pat's throat."

"Wouldn't it be awful if—if anything happened to Pat?" whispered Cecily.

"Well, we could have a jolly funeral, you know," said Dan.

We looked at him in such horror that Dan hastened to apologize.

"I'd be awful sorry myself if Pat died. But if he *did*, we'd

have to give him the right kind of a funeral," he protested.
"Why, Paddy just seems like one of the family."

The Story Girl finished her turnover, and stretched herself
out on the grasses, pillowing her chin in her hands and looking
at the sky. She was bare headed, as usual, and her scarlet ribbon
was bound filletwise about her head. She had twined freshly
plucked dandelions around it and the effect was that of a crown
of brilliant golden stars on her sleek, brown curls.

"Look at that long, thin, lacy cloud up there," she said.
"What does it make you think of, girls?"

"A wedding veil," said Cecily.

"That is just what it is—the Wedding Veil of the Proud
Princess. I know a story about it. I read it in a book. Once upon
a time"—the Story Girl's eyes grew dreamy, and her accents
floated away on the summer air like wind-blown rose petals—
"there was a princess who was the most beautiful princess in the
world, and kings from all lands came to woo her for a bride. But
she was as proud as she was beautiful. She laughed all her suitors
to scorn. And when her father urged her to choose one of them
as her husband she drew herself up haughtily—so—"

The Story Girl sprang to her feet and for a moment we saw
the proud princess of the old tale in all her scornful loveliness—
"and she said,

" 'I will not wed until a king comes who can conquer all
kings. Then I shall be the wife of the king of the world and no
one can hold herself higher than I.'

"So every king went to war to prove that he could conquer
every one else, and there was a great deal of bloodshed and
misery. But the proud princess laughed and sang, and she and
her maidens worked at a wonderful lace veil which she meant to
wear when the king of all kings came. It was a very beautiful
veil; but her maidens whispered that a man had died and a
woman's heart had broken for every stitch set in it.

"Just when a king thought he had conquered everybody
some other king would come and conquer *him;* and so it went on
until it did not seem likely the proud princess would ever get a
husband at all. But still her pride was so great that she would
not yield, even though everybody except the kings who wanted
to marry her, hated her for the suffering she had caused. One day
a horn was blown at the palace gate; and there was one tall man
in complete armor, with his visor down, riding on a white horse.

When he said he had come to marry the princess every one laughed, for he had no retinue and no beautiful apparel, and no golden crown.

" 'But I am the king who conquers all kings,' he said.

" 'You must prove it before I shall marry you,' said the proud princess. But she trembled and turned pale, for there was something in his voice that frightened her. And when he laughed, his laughter was still more dreadful.

" 'I can easily prove it, beautiful princess,' he said, 'but you must go with me to my kingdom for the proof. Marry me now; and you and I and your father and all your court will ride straightway to my kingdom; and if you are not satisfied then that I am the king who conquers all kings you may give me back my ring and return home free of me forever more.'

"It was a strange wooing and the friends of the princess begged her to refuse. But her pride whispered that it would be such a wonderful thing to be the queen of the king of the world; so she consented; and her maidens dressed her, and put on the long lace veil that had been so many years a-making. Then they were married at once, but the bridegroom never lifted his visor and no one saw his face. The proud princess held herself more proudly than ever, but she was as white as her veil. And there was no laughter or merry-making, such as should be at a wedding, and every one looked at every one else with fear in his eyes.

"After the wedding the bridegroom lifted his bride before him on his white horse, and her father and all the members of his court mounted, too, and rode after them. On and on they rode, and the skies grew darker and the wind blew and wailed, and the shades of evening came down. And just in the twilight they rode into a dark valley, filled with tombs and graves.

" 'Why have you brought me here?' cried the proud princess angrily.

" 'This is my kingdom,' he answered. 'These are the tombs of the kings I have conquered. Behold me, beautiful princess. I am Death!'

"He lifted his visor. All saw his awful face. The proud princess shrieked.

" 'Come to my arms, my bride,' he cried. 'I have won you fairly. I am the king who conquers all kings!'

"He clasped her fainting form to his breast and spurred his

white horse to the tombs. A tempest of rain broke over the valley and blotted them from sight. Very sadly the old king and courtiers rode home, and never, never again did human eye behold the proud princess. But when those long, white clouds sweep across the sky, the country people in the land where she lived say 'Look you, there is the Wedding Veil of the Proud Princess.'"

The weird spell of the tale rested on us for some moments after the Story Girl had finished. We had walked with her in the place of death and grown cold with the horror that chilled the heart of the poor princess. Dan presently broke the spell.

"You see it doesn't do to be too proud, Felicity," he remarked, giving her a poke. "You'd better not say too much about Peter's patches."

# CHAPTER V

## *Peter Goes to Church*

THERE was no Sunday School the next afternoon, as superintendent and teachers wished to attend a communion service at Markdale. The Carlisle service was in the evening, and at sunset we were waiting at Uncle Alec's front door for Peter and the Story Girl.

None of the grown-ups were going to church. Aunt Olivia had a sick headache and Uncle Roger stayed home with her. Aunt Janet and Uncle Alec had gone to the Markdale service and had not yet returned.

Felicity and Cecily were wearing their new summer muslins for the first time—and were acutely conscious of the fact. Felicity, her pink and white face shadowed by her drooping, forget-me-not-wreathed, leghorn hat, was as beautiful as usual; but Cecily, having tortured her hair with curl papers all night, had a rampant bush of curls all about her head which quite destroyed the sweet, nun-like expression of her little features. Cecily cherished a grudge against fate because she had not been given naturally curly hair as had the other two girls. But she attained the desire of her heart on Sundays at least, and was quite well satisfied. It was imposible to convince her that the satin smooth lustre of her week-day tresses was much more becoming to her.

Presently Peter and the Story Girl appeared, and we were all more or less relieved to see that Peter looked quite respectable, despite the indisputable patch on his trousers. His face was rosy, his thick black curls were smoothly combed, and his tie was neatly bowed; but it was his legs which we scrutinized most anxiously. At first glance they seemed well enough; but closer inspection revealed something not altogether customary.

"What is the matter with your stockings, Peter?" asked Dan bluntly.

"Oh, I hadn't a pair without holes in the legs," answered Peter easily, "because ma hadn't time to darn them this week. So I put on two pairs. The holes don't come in the same places, and you'd never notice them unless you looked right close."

"Have you got a cent for collection?" demanded Felicity.

"I've got a Yankee cent. I s'pose it will do, won't it?"

Felicity shook her head vehemently.

"Oh, no, no. It may be all right to pass a Yankee cent on a store keeper or an egg peddler, but it would never do for church."

"I'll have to go without any, then," said Peter. "I haven't another cent. I only get fifty cents a week and I give it all to ma last night."

But Peter must have a cent. Felicity would have given him one herself—and she was none too lavish of her coppers—rather than have him go without one. Dan, however, lent him one, on the distinct understanding that it was to be repaid the next week.

Uncle Roger wandered by at this moment and, beholding Peter, said,

"'Is Saul also among the prophets?' What can have induced you to turn church-goer, Peter, when all Olivia's gentle persuasions were of no avail? The old, old argument I suppose—'beauty draws us with a single hair.'"

Uncle Roger looked quizzically at Felicity. We did not know what his quotations meant, but we understood he thought Peter was going to church because of Felicity. Felicity tossed her head.

"It isn't my fault that he's going to church," she said snappishly. "It's the Story Girl's doings."

Uncle Roger sat down on the doorstep, and gave himself over to one of the silent, inward paroxysms of laughter we all found so very aggravating. He shook his big, blond head, shut his eyes, and murmured,

"Not her fault! Oh, Felicity, Felicity, you'll be the death of your dear Uncle yet if you don't watch out."

Felicity started off indignantly, and we followed, picking up Sara Ray at the foot of the hill.

The Carlisle church was a very old-fashioned one, with a square, ivy-hung tower. It was shaded by tall elms, and the graveyard surrounded it completely, many of the graves being directly under its windows. We always took the corner path through it, passing the King plot where our kindred of four generations slept in a green solitude of wavering light and shadow.

There was Great-grandfather King's flat tombstone of rough Island sandstone, so overgrown with ivy that we could hardly read its lengthy inscription, recording his whole history in brief, and finishing with eight lines of original verse composed by his widow. I do not think that poetry was Great-grandmother King's strong point. When Felix read it, on our first Sunday in Carlisle, he remarked dubiously that it *looked* like poetry but didn't *sound* like it.

There, too, slept the Emily whose faithful spirit was supposed to haunt the orchard; but Edith who had kissed the poet lay not with her kindred. She had died in a far, foreign land, and the murmur of an alien sea sounded about her grave.

White marble tablets, ornamented with weeping willow trees, marked where Grandfather and Grandmother King were buried, and a single shaft of red Scotch granite stood between the graves of Aunt Felicity and Uncle Felix. The Story Girl lingered to lay a bunch of wild violets, misty blue and faintly sweet, on her mother's grave; and then she read aloud the verse on the stone.

" 'They were lovely and pleasant in their lives and in their death they were not divided.' "

The tones of her voice brought out the poignant and immortal beauty and pathos of that wonderful old lament. The girls wiped their eyes; and we boys felt as if we might have done so, too, had nobody been looking. What better epitaph could any one wish than to have it said that he was lovely and pleasant in his life? When I heard the Story Girl read it I made a secret compact with myself that I would try to deserve such an epitaph.

"I wish I had a family plot," said Peter, rather wistfully. "I haven't *anything* you fellows have. The Craigs are just buried anywhere they happen to die."

"I'd like to be buried here when I die," said Felix. "But I hope it won't be for a good while yet," he added in a livelier tone, as we moved onward to the church.

The interior of the church was as old-fashioned as its

exterior. It was furnished with square box pews; the pulpit was a "wine-glass" one, and was reached by a steep, narrow flight of steps. Uncle Alec's pew was at the top of the church, quite near the pulpit.

Peter's appearance did not attract as much attention as we had fondly expected. Indeed, nobody seemed to notice him at all. The lamps were not yet lighted and the church was filled with a soft twilight and hush. Outside, the sky was purple and gold and silvery green, with a delicate tangle of rosy cloud above the elms.

"Isn't it awful nice and holy in here?" whispered Peter reverently. "I didn't know church was like this. It's nice."

Felicity frowned at him, and the Story Girl touched him with her slippered foot to remind him that he must not talk in church. Peter stiffened up and sat at attention during the service. Nobody could have behaved better. But when the sermon was over and the collection was being taken up, he made the sensation which his entrance had not produced.

Elder Frewen, a tall, pale man, with long, sandy side-whiskers, appeared at the door of our pew with the collection plate. We knew Elder Frewen quite well and liked him; he was Aunt Janet's cousin and often visited her. The contrast between his week-day jollity and the unearthly solemnity of his countenance on Sundays always struck us as very funny. It seemed so to strike Peter; for as Peter dropped his cent into the plate he laughed aloud!

Everybody looked at our pew. I have always wondered why Felicity did not die of mortification on the spot. The Story Girl turned white, and Cecily turned red. As for that poor, unlucky Peter, the shame of his countenance was pitiful to behold. He never lifted his head for the remainder of the service; and he followed us down the aisle and across the graveyard like a beaten dog. None of us uttered a word until we reached the road, lying in the white moonshine of the May night. Then Felicity broke the tense silence by remarking to the Story Girl,

"I told you so!"

The Story Girl made no response. Peter sidled up to her.

"I'm awful sorry," he said contritely. "I never meant to laugh. It just happened before I could stop myself. It was this way—"

"Don't you ever speak to me again," said the Story Girl, in a tone of cold concentrated fury. "Go and be a Methodist, or a Mohammedan, or *anything*! I don't care what you are! You have *humiliated* me!"

She marched off with Sara Ray, and Peter dropped back to us with a frightened face.

"What is it I've done to her?" he whispered. "What does that big word mean?"

"Oh, never mind," I said crossly—for I felt that Peter *had* disgraced us—"She's just mad—and no wonder. Whatever made you act so crazy, Peter?"

"Well, I didn't mean to. And I wanted to laugh twice before that and *didn't*. It was the Story Girl's stories made me want to laugh, so I don't think it's fair for her to be mad at me. She hadn't ought to tell me stories about people if she don't want me to laugh when I see them. When I looked at Samuel Ward I thought of him getting up in meeting one night, and praying that he might be guided in his upsetting and downrising. I remembered the way she took him off, and I wanted to laugh. And then I looked at the pulpit and thought of the story she told about the old Scotch minister who was too fat to get in at the door of it, and had to h'ist himself by his two hands over it, and then whispered to the other minister so that everybody heard him,

"'*This pulpit door was made for speerits*'—and I wanted to laugh. And then Mr. Frewen come—and I thought of her story about his sidewhiskers—how when his first wife died of information of the lungs he went courting Celia Ward, and Celia told him she wouldn't marry him unless he shaved them whiskers off. And he wouldn't, just to be stubborn. And one day one of them caught fire, when he was burning brush, and burned off, and every one thought he'd *have* to shave the other off then. But he didn't, and just went round with one whisker till the burned one grew out. And then Celia give in and took him, because she saw there wasn't no hope of *him* ever giving in. I just remembered that story, and I thought I could see him, taking up the cents so solemn, with one long whisker; and the laugh just laughed itself before I could help it."

We all exploded with laughter on the spot, much to the horror of Mrs. Abraham Ward, who was just driving past, and who came up the next day and told Aunt Janet we had "acted scandalous" on the road home from church. We felt ashamed ourselves, for we knew people should conduct themselves decently and in order on Sunday farings-forth. But, as with Peter, it "had laughed itself."

Even Felicity laughed. Felicity was not nearly so angry with Peter as might have been expected. She even walked beside him and let him carry her Bible. They talked quite confidentially. Perhaps she forgave him the more easily, because he had justified her in her predictions, and thus afforded her a decided triumph over the Story Girl.

"I'm going to keep on going to church," Peter told her. "I like it. Sermons are more int'resting than I thought, and I like the singing. I wish I could make up my mind whether to be a Presbyterian or a Methodist. I s'pose I might ask the minister about it."

"Oh, no, no, don't do that," said Felicity in alarm. "Ministers wouldn't want to be bothered with such questions."

"Why not? What are ministers for if they ain't to tell people how to get to heaven?"

"Oh, well, it's all right for grown-ups to ask them things, of course. But it isn't respectful for little boys—especially hired boys."

"I don't see why. But anyhow, I s'pose it wouldn't be much use, because if he was a Presbyterian minister he'd say I ought to be a Presbyterian, and if he was a Methodist he'd tell me to be one, too. Look here, Felicity, what *is* the difference between them?"

"I—I don't know," said Felicity reluctantly. "I s'pose children can't understand such things. There must be a great deal of difference, of course, if we only knew what it was. Anyhow, *I* am a Presbyterian, and I'm glad of it."

We walked on in silence for a time, thinking our own young thoughts. Presently they were scattered by an abrupt and startling question from Peter.

"What does God look like?" he said.

It appeared that none of us had any idea.

"The Story Girl would prob'ly know," said Cecily.

"I wish I knew," said Peter gravely. "I wish I could see a picture of God. It would make Him seem lots more real."

"I've often wondered myself what He looks like," said Felicity in a burst of confidence. Even in Felicity, so it would seem, there were depths of thought unplumbed.

"I've seen pictures of Jesus," said Felix meditatively. "He looks just like a man, only better and kinder. But now that I come to think of it, I've never seen a picture of God."

"Well, if there isn't one in Toronto it isn't likely there's one anywhere," said Peter disappointedly. "I saw a picture of the devil once," he added. "It was in a book my Aunt Jane had. She got it for a prize in school. My Aunt Jane was clever."

"It couldn't have been a very good book if there was such a picture in it," said Felicity.

"It was a real good book. My Aunt Jane wouldn't have a book that wasn't good," retorted Peter sulkily.

He refused to discuss the subject further, somewhat to our disappointment. For we had never seen a picture of the person referred to, and we were rather curious regarding it.

"We'll ask Peter to describe it sometime when he's in a better humour," whispered Felix.

Sara Ray having turned in at her own gate, I ran ahead to join the Story Girl, and we walked up the hill together. She had recovered her calmness of mind, but she made no reference to Peter. When we reached our lane and passed under Grandfather King's big willow the fragrance of the orchard struck us in the face like a wave. We could see the long rows of trees, a white gladness in the moonshine. It seemed to us that there was in the orchard something different from other orchards that we had known. We were too young to analyze the vague sensation. In later years we were to understand that it was because the orchard blossomed not only apple blossoms but all the love, faith, joy, pure happiness and pure sorrow of those who had made it and walked there.

"The orchard doesn't seem the same place by moonlight at all," said the Story Girl dreamily. "It's lovely, but it's different. When I was very small I used to believe the fairies danced in it on moonlight nights. I would like to believe it now but I can't."

"Why not?"

"Oh, it's so hard to believe things you know are not true. It was Uncle Edward who told me there were no such things as fairies. I was just seven. He is a minister, so of course I knew he spoke the truth. It was his duty to tell me, and I do not blame him, but I have never felt quite the same to Uncle Edward since."

Ah, do we ever "feel quite the same" towards people who

destroy our illusions? Shall I ever be able to forgive the brutal
creature who first told me there was no person as Santa Claus?
He was a boy, three years older than myself; and he may now, for
aught I know, be a most useful and respectable member of
society, beloved by his kind. But I know what he must ever
seem to me!

We waited at Uncle Alec's door for the others to come up.
Peter was by way of skulking shamefacedly past into the
shadows; but the Story Girl's brief, bitter anger had vanished.

"Wait for me, Peter," she called.

She went over to him and held out her hand.

"I forgive you," she said graciously.

Felix and I felt that it would really be worth while to offend
her, just to be forgiven in such an adorable voice. Peter eagerly
grasped her hand.

"I tell you what, Story Girl, I'm awful sorry I laughed in
church, but you needn't be afraid I ever will again. No, sir! And
I'm going to church and Sunday School regular, and I'll say my
prayers every night. I want to be like the rest of you. And look
here! I've thought of the way my Aunt Jane used to give
medicine to a cat. You mix the powder in lard, and spread it on
his paws and his sides and he'll lick it off, 'cause a cat can't stand
being messy. If Paddy isn't any better to-morrow we'll do that."

They went away together hand in hand, children-wise, up
the lane of spruces crossed with bars of moonlight. And there
was peace over all that fresh and flowery land, and peace in our
little hearts.

# CHAPTER VI

# The Mystery of Golden Milestone

PADDY was smeared with medicated lard the next day, all of us assisting at the rite, although the Story Girl was high priestess. Then, out of regard for mats and cushions, he was kept in durance vile in the granary until he had licked his fur clean. This treatment being repeated every day for a week, Pat recovered his usual health and spirits, and our minds were set at rest to enjoy the next excitement—collecting for a school library fund.

Our teacher thought it would be an excellent thing to have a library in connection with the school; and he suggested that each of the pupils should try to see how much money he or she could raise for the project during the month of June. We might earn it by honest toil, or gather it in by contributions levied on our friends.

The result was a determined rivalry as to which pupil should collect the largest sum; and this rivalry was especially intense in our home coterie.

Our relatives started us with a quarter apiece. For the rest, we knew we must depend on our own exertions. Peter was handicapped at the beginning by the fact that he had no family friend to finance him.

"If my Aunt Jane'd been living she'd have given me something," he remarked. "And if my father hadn't run away he might have given me something too. But I'm going to do the best I can anyhow. Your Aunt Olivia says I can have the job of gathering the eggs, and I'm to have one egg out of every dozen to sell for myself."

Felicity made a similar bargain with her mother. The Story

Girl and Cecily were each to be paid ten cents a week for washing dishes in their respective homes. Felix and Dan contracted to keep the gardens free from weeds. I caught brook trout in the westering valley of spruces and sold them for a cent apiece.

Sara Ray was the only unhappy one among us. She could do nothing. She had no relatives in Carlisle except her mother, and her mother did not approve of the school library project, and would not give Sara a cent, or put her in any way of earning one. To Sara, this was humiliation indescribable. She felt herself an outcast and an alien to our busy little circle, where each member counted every day, with miserly delight, his slowly increasing hoard of small cash.

"I'm just going to pray to God to send me some money," she announced desperately at last.

"I don't believe that'll do any good," said Dan. "He gives lots of things, but He doesn't give money, because people can earn that for themselves."

"*I* can't," said Sara, with passionate defiance. "I think He ought to take that into account."

"Don't worry, dear," said Cecily, who always poured balm. "If you can't collect any money everybody will know it isn't your fault."

"I won't ever feel like reading a single book in the library if I can't give something to it," mourned Sara.

Dan and the girls and I were sitting in a row on Aunt Olivia's garden fence, watching Felix weed. Felix worked well, although he did not like weeding—"fat boys never do," Felicity informed him. Felix pretended not to hear her, but I knew he did, because his ears grew red. Felix's face never blushed, but his ears always gave him away. As for Felicity, she did not say things like that out of malice prepense. It never occurred to her that Felix did not like to be called fat.

"I always feel so sorry for the poor weeds," said the Story Girl dreamily. "It must be very hard to be rooted up."

"They shouldn't grow in the wrong place," said Felicity mercilessly.

"When weeds go to heaven I suppose they will be flowers," continued the Story Girl.

"You do think such queer things," said Felicity.

"A rich man in Toronto has a floral clock in his garden," I

said. "It looks just like the face of a clock, and there are flowers in it that open at every hour, so that you can always tell the time."

"Oh, I wish we had one here," exclaimed Cecily.

"What would be the use of it?" asked the Story Girl a little disdainfully. "Nobody ever wants to know the time in a garden."

I slipped away at this point, suddenly remembering that it was time to take a dose of magic seed. I had bought it from Billy Robinson three days before in school. Billy had assured me that it would make me grow faster.

I was beginning to feel secretly worried because I did not grow. I had overheard Aunt Janet say I was going to be short, like Uncle Alec. Now, I loved Uncle Alec, but I wanted to be taller than he was. So when Billy confided to me, under solemn promise of secrecy, that he had some "magic seed," which would make boys grow, and would sell me a box of it for ten cents, I jumped at the offer. Billy was taller than any boy of his age in Carlisle, and he assured me it all came from taking magic seed.

"I was a regular runt before I begun," he said, "and look at me now. I got it from Peg Bowen. She's a witch, you know. I wouldn't go near her again for a bushel of magic seed. It was an awful experience. I haven't much left, but I guess I've enough to do me till I'm as tall as I want to be. You must take a pinch of the seed every three hours, walking backward, and you must never tell a soul you're taking it, or it won't work. I wouldn't spare any of it to anyone but you."

I felt deeply grateful to Billy, and sorry that I had not liked him better. Somehow, nobody did like Billy Robinson over and above. But I vowed I *would* like him in future. I paid him the ten cents cheerfully and took the magic seed as directed, measuring myself carefully every day by a mark on the hall door. I could not see any advance in growth yet, but then I had been taking it only three days.

One day the Story Girl had an inspiration.

"Let us go and ask the Awkward Man and Mr. Campbell for a contribution to the library fund," she said. "I am sure no one else has asked them, because nobody in Carlisle is related to them. Let us all go, and if they give us anything we'll divide it equally among us."

It was a daring proposition, for both Mr. Campbell and the Awkward Man were regarded as eccentric personages; and Mr.

Campbell was supposed to detest children. But where the Story Girl led we would follow to the death. The next day being Saturday, we started out in the afternoon.

We took a short cut to Golden Milestone, over a long, green, dewy land full of placid meadows, where sunshine had fallen asleep. At first all was not harmonious. Felicity was in an ill humour; she had wanted to wear her second best dress, and Aunt Janet had decreed that her school clothes were good enough to go "traipsing about in the dust." Then the Story Girl arrived, arrayed not in any second best but in her very best dress and hat, which her father had sent her from Paris—a dress of soft, crimson silk, and a white leghorn hat encircled by flame-red poppies. Neither Felicity nor Cecily could have worn it; but it became the Story Girl perfectly. In it she was a thing of fire and laughter and glow, as if the singular charm of her temperament were visible and tangible in its vivid colouring and silken texture.

"I shouldn't think you'd put on your best clothes to go begging for the library in," said Felicity cuttingly.

"Aunt Olivia says that when you are going to have an important interview with a man you ought to look your very best," said the Story Girl, giving her skirt a lustrous swirl and enjoying the effect.

"Aunt Olivia spoils you," said Felicity.

"She doesn't, either, Felicity King! Aunt Olivia is just sweet. She kisses me good-night every night, and your mother *never* kisses you."

"My mother doesn't make kisses so common," retorted Felicity. "But she gives us pie for dinner every day."

"So does Aunt Olivia."

"Yes, but look at the difference in the size of the pieces! And Aunt Olivia only gives you skim milk. My mother gives us cream."

"Aunt Olivia's skim milk is as good as your mother's cream," cried the Story Girl hotly.

"Oh, girls, don't fight," said Cecily, the peacemaker. "It's such a nice day, and we'll have a nice time if you don't spoil it by fighting."

"We're *not* fighting," said Felicity. "And I like Aunt Olivia. But my mother is just as good as Aunt Olivia, there now!"

"Of course she is. Aunt Janet is splendid," agreed the Story Girl.

They smiled at each other amicably. Felicity and the Story Girl were really quite fond of each other, under the queer surface friction that commonly resulted from their intercourse.

"You said once you knew a story about the Awkward Man," said Felix. "You might tell it to us."

"All right," agreed the Story Girl. "The only trouble is, I don't know the whole story. But I'll tell you all I do know. I call it 'The Mystery of Golden Milestone.'"

"Oh, I don't believe that story is true," said Felicity. "I believe Mrs. Griggs was just romancing. She *does* romance, mother says."

"Yes; but I don't believe she could ever have thought of such a thing as this herself, so I believe it must be true," said the Story Girl. "Anyway, this is the story, boys. You know the Awkward Man has lived alone ever since his mother died, ten years ago. Abel Griggs is his hired man, and he and his wife live in a little house down the Awkward Man's lane. Mrs. Griggs makes his bread for him, and she cleans up his house now and then. She says he keeps it very neat. But till last fall there was one room she never saw. It was always locked—the west one, looking out over his garden. One day last fall the Awkward Man went to Summerside, and Mrs. Griggs scrubbed his kitchen. Then she went over the whole house and she tried the door of the west room. Mrs. Griggs is a *very* curious woman. Uncle Roger says all women have as much curiosity as is good for them, but Mrs. Griggs has more. She expected to find the door locked as usual. It was *not* locked. She opened it and went in. What do you suppose she found?"

"Something like—like Bluebeard's chamber?" suggested Felix in a scared tone.

"Oh, no, *no*! Nothing like *that* could happen in Prince Edward Island. But if there *had* been beautiful wives hanging up by their hair all round the walls I don't believe Mrs. Griggs could have been much more astonished. The room had never been furnished in his mother's time, but now it was *elegantly* furnished, though Mrs. Griggs says *she* doesn't know when or how that furniture was brought there. She says she never saw a room like it in a country farmhouse. It was like a bed-room and sitting-room combined. The floor was covered with a carpet like green velvet. There were fine lace curtains at the windows and beautiful pictures on the walls. There was a little white bed, and a dressing-table, a bookcase full of books, a stand with a work basket on it, and a rocking-chair. There was a woman's picture above the bookcase. Mrs. Griggs says she thinks it was a coloured photograph, but she didn't know who it was. Anyway, it was a very pretty girl. But the most amazing thing of all was that *a woman's dress* was hanging over a chair by the table. Mrs. Griggs says it *never* belonged to Jasper Dale's mother, for she thought it a sin to wear anything but print and drugget; and this dress was of *pale blue* silk. Besides that, there was a pair of blue satin slippers on the floor beside it—*high-heeled* slippers. And on the fly-leaves of all the books the name 'Alice' was written. Now, there never was an Alice in the Dale connection, and nobody ever heard of the Awkward Man having a sweetheart. There, isn't that a lovely mystery?"

"It's a pretty queer yarn," said Felix. "I wonder if it is true—and what it means."

"I intend to find out what it means," said the Story Girl. "I am going to get acquainted with the Awkward Man sometime, and then I'll find out his Alice-secret."

"I don't see how you'll ever get acquainted with him," said Felicity. "He never goes anywhere except to church. He just stays home and reads books when he isn't working. Mother says he is a perfect hermit."

"I'll manage it somehow," said the Story Girl—and we had no doubt that she would. "But I must wait till I'm a little older, for he wouldn't tell the secret of the west room to a little girl. And I mustn't wait till I'm *too* old, for he is frightened of grown-up girls, because he thinks they laugh at his awkwardness. I know I will like him. He has such a nice face, even if he is awkward. He looks like a man you could tell things to."

"Well, I'd like a man who could move around without falling over his own feet," said Felicity. "And then the look of him! Uncle Roger says he is long, lank, lean, narrow, and contracted."

"Things always sound worse than they are when Uncle Roger says them," said the Story Girl. "Uncle Edwards says Jasper Dale is a very clever man and it's a great pity he wasn't able to finish his college course. He went to college two years, you know. Then his father died, and he stayed home with his mother because she was very delicate. *I* call him a hero. I wonder if it is true that he writes poetry. Mrs. Griggs says it is. She says she has seen him writing it in a brown book. She said she couldn't get near enough to read it, but she knew it was poetry by the shape of it."

"Very likely. If that blue silk dress story is true, I'd believe *anything* of him," said Felicity.

We were near Golden Milestone now. The house was a big, weather-gray structure, overgrown with vines and climbing roses. Something about the three square windows in the second story gave it an appearance of winking at us in a friendly fashion through its vines—at least, so the Story Girl said; and, indeed, we could see if for ourselves after she had once pointed it out to us.

We did not get into the house, however. We met the Awkward Man in his yard, and he gave us a quarter apiece for our library. He did not seem awkward or shy; but then we were only children, and his foot was on his native heath.

He was a tall, slender man, who did not look his forty years, so unwrinkled was his high, white forehead, so clear and lustrous his large, dark-blue eyes, so free from silver threads his rather long black hair. He had large hands and feet, and walked with a slight stoop. I am afraid we stared at him rather rudely while the Story Girl talked to him. But was not an Awkward Man, who was also a hermit and kept blue silk dresses in a locked room, and possibly wrote poetry, a legitimate object of curiosity? I leave it to you.

When we got away we compared notes, and found that we all liked him—and this, although he had said little and had appeared somewhat glad to get rid of us.

"He gave us the money like a gentleman," said the Story Girl. "I felt he didn't grudge it. And now for Mr. Campbell. It was on *his* account I put on my red silk. I don't suppose the Awkward Man noticed it at all, but Mr. Campbell will, or I'm much mistaken."

# CHAPTER VII

## How
## Betty
## Sherman
## Won a
## Husband

THE rest of us did not share the Story Girl's enthusiasm regarding our call on Mr. Campbell. We secretly dreaded it. If, as was said, he detested children, who knew what sort of a reception we might meet?

Mr. Campbell was a rich, retired farmer, who took life easily. He had visited New York and Boston, Toronto and Montreal; he had even been as far as the Pacific coast. Therefore he was regarded in Carlisle as a much travelled man; and he was known to be "well read" and intelligent. But it was also known that Mr. Campbell was not always in a good humour. If he liked you there was nothing he would not do for you; if he disliked you—well, you were not left in ignorance of it. In short, we had the impression that Mr. Campbell resembled the famous little girl with the curl in the middle of her forehead. "When he was good, he was very, very good, and when he was bad he was horrid." What if this were one of his horrid days?

"He can't *do* anything to us, you know," said the Story Girl. "He may be rude, but that won't hurt any one but himself."

"Hard words break no bones," observed Felix philosophically.

"But they hurt your feelings. *I* am afraid of Mr. Campbell," said Cecily candidly.

"Perhaps we'd better give up and go home," suggested Dan.

"You can go home if you like," said the Story Girl scornfully. "But *I* am going to see Mr. Campbell. I know I can manage him. But if I have to go alone, and he gives me anything, I'll keep it all for my own collection, mind you."

That settled it. We were not going to let the Story Girl get ahead of us in the matter of collecting.

Mr. Campbell's housekeeper ushered us into his parlour and left us. Presently Mr. Campbell himself was standing in the doorway, looking us over. We took heart of grace. It seemed to be one of his good days, for there was a quizzical smile on his broad, clean-shaven, strongly-featured face. Mr. Campbell was a tall man, with a massive head, well thatched with thick, black hair, gray-streaked. He had big, black eyes, with many wrinkles around them, and a thin, firm, long-lipped mouth. We thought him handsome, for an old man.

His gaze wandered over us with uncomplimentary indifference until it fell on the Story Girl, leaning back in an armchair. She looked like a slender red lily in the unstudied grace of her attitude. A spark flashed into Mr. Campbell's black eyes.

"Is this a Sunday School deputation?" he inquired rather ironically.

"No. We have come to ask a favour of you," said the Story Girl.

The magic of her voice worked its will on Mr. Campbell, as on all others. He came in, sat down, hooked his thumb into his vest pocket, and smiled at her.

"What is it?" he asked.

"We are collecting for our school library, and we have called to ask you for a contribution," she replied.

"Why should *I* contribute to your school library?" demanded Mr. Campbell.

This was a poser for us. Why should he, indeed? But the Story Girl was quite equal to it. Leaning forward, and throwing an indescribable witchery into tone and eyes and smile, she said,

"Because a lady asks you."

Mr. Campbell chuckled.

"The best of all reasons," he said. "But see here, my dear young lady, I'm an old miser and curmudgeon, as you may have heard. I *hate* to part with my money, even for a good reason. And I *never* part with any of it, unless I am to receive some benefit from the expenditure. Now, what earthly good could I get from your three by six school library? None whatever. But I shall make you a fair offer. I have heard from my housekeeper's urchin of a son that you are a 'master hand' to tell stories. Tell me one, here and now. I shall pay you in proportion to the entertainment you afford me. Come now, and do your prettiest."

There was a fine mockery in his tone that put the Story Girl on her mettle instantly. She sprang to her feet, an amazing change coming over her. Her eyes flashed and burned; crimson spots glowed in her cheeks.

"I shall tell you the story of the Sherman girls, and how Betty Sherman won a husband," she said.

We gasped. Was the Story Girl crazy? Or had she forgotten that Betty Sherman was Mr. Campbell's own great-grandmother, and that her method of winning a husband was not exactly in accordance with maidenly traditions.

But Mr. Campbell chuckled again.

"An excellent test," he said. "If you can amuse *me* with that story you must be a wonder. I've heard it so often that it has no more interest for me than the alphabet."

"One cold winter day, eighty years ago," began the Story Girl without further parley, "Donald Fraser was sitting by the window of his new house, playing his fiddle for company, and looking out over the white, frozen bay before his door. It was bitter, bitter cold, and a storm was brewing. But, storm, or no storm, Donald meant to go over the bay that evening to see Nancy Sherman. He was thinking of her as he played 'Annie Laurie,' for Nancy was more beautiful than the lady of the song. 'Her face, it is the fairest that e'er the sun shone on,' hummed Donald—and oh, he thought so, too! He did not know whether Nancy cared for him or not. He had many rivals. But he knew that if she would not come to be the mistress of his new house no one else ever should. So he sat there that afternoon and dreamed of her, as he played sweet old songs and rollicking jigs on his fiddle.

"While he was playing a sleigh drove up to the door, and Neil Campbell came in. Donald was not overly glad to see him, for he suspected where he was going. Neil Campbell, who was Highland Scotch and lived down at Berwick, was courting Nancy Sherman, too; and, what was far worse, Nancy's father favoured him, because he was a richer man than Donald Fraser.

But Donald was not going to show all he thought—Scotch people never do—and he pretended to be very glad to see Neil, and made him heartily welcome.

"Neil sat down by the roaring fire, looking quite well satisfied with himself. It was ten miles from Berwick to the bay shore, and a call at a half way house was just the thing. Then Donald brought out the whisky. They always did that eighty years ago, you know. If you were a woman, you could give your visitors a dish of tea; but if you were a man and did not offer them a 'taste' of whisky, you were thought either very mean or very ignorant.

"'You look cold,' said Donald, in his great, hearty voice. 'Sit nearer the fire, man, and put a bit of warmth in your veins. It's bitter cold the day. And now tell me the Berwick news. Has Jean McLean made up with her man yet? And is it true that Sandy McQuarrie is to marry Kate Ferguson? 'Twill be a match now! Sure, with her red hair, Sandy will not be like to lose his bride past finding.'

"Neil had plenty of news to tell. And the more whisky he drank the more he told. He didn't notice that Donald was not taking much. Neil talked on and on, and of course he soon began to tell things it would have been much wiser not to tell. Finally he told Donald that he was going over the bay to ask Nancy Sherman that very night to marry him. And if she would have him, then Donald and all the folks should see a wedding that *was* a wedding.

"Oh, wasn't Donald taken aback! This was more than he had expected. Neil hadn't been courting Nancy very long, and Donald never dreamed he would propose to her *quite* so soon.

"At first Donald didn't know what to do. He felt sure deep down in his heart, that Nancy liked *him*. She was very shy and modest, but you know a girl can let a man see she likes him without going out of her way. But Donald knew that if Neil proposed first he would have the best chance. Neil was rich and the Shermans were poor, and old Elias Sherman would have the most to say in the matter. If he told Nancy she must take Neil Campbell she would never dream of disobeying him. Old Elias Sherman was a man who had to be obeyed. But if Nancy had only promised some one else first her father would not make her break her word.

"Wasn't it a hard plight for poor Donald? But he was a Scotchman, you know, and it's pretty hard to stick a Scotchman long. Presently a twinkle came into his eyes, for he remembered that all was fair in love and war. So he said to Neil, oh, so persuasively,

" 'Have some more, man, have some more. 'Twill keep the heart in you in the teeth of that wind. Help yourself. There's plenty more where that came from.'

"Neil didn't want *much* persuasion. He took some more, and said slyly,

" 'Is it going over the bay the night that yourself will be doing?'

"Donald shook his head.

" 'I had thought of it,' he owned, 'but it looks a wee like a storm, and my sleigh is at the blacksmith's to be shod. If I went it must be on Black Dan's back, and he likes a canter over the ice in a snow-storm as little as I. His own fireside is the best place for a man to-night, Campbell. Have another taste, man, have another taste.'

"Neil went on 'tasting,' and that sly Donald sat there with a sober face, but laughing eyes, and coaxed him on. At last Neil's head fell forward on his breast, and he was sound asleep. Donald got up, put on his overcoat and cap, and went to the door.

" 'May your sleep be long and sweet, man,' he said, laughing softly, 'and as for the waking, 'twill be betwixt you and me.'

"With that he untied Neil's horse, climbed into Neil's sleigh, and tucked Neil's buffalo robe about him.

" 'Now, Bess, old girl, do your bonniest,' he said. 'There's more than you know hangs on your speed. If the Campbell wakes too soon Black Dan could show you a pair of clean heels for all your good start. On, my girl.'

"Brown Bess went over the ice like a deer, and Donald kept thinking of what he should say to Nancy—and more still of what she would say to him. *Suppose* he was mistaken. *Suppose* she said 'no!'

" 'Neil will have the laugh on me then. Sure he's sleeping well. And the snow is coming soon. There'll be a bonny swirl on the bay ere long. I hope no harm will come to the lad if he starts to cross. When he wakes up he'll be in such a fine Highland temper that he'll never stop to think of danger. Well, Bess, old girl, here we are. Now, Donald Fraser, pluck up heart and play the man. Never flinch because a slip of a lass looks scornful at you out of the bonniest dark-blue eyes on earth.'

"But in spite of his bold words Donald's heart was thumping as he drove into the Sherman yard. Nancy was there, milking a cow by the stable door, but she stood up when she saw Donald coming. Oh, she was very beautiful! Her hair was like a skein of golden silk, and her eyes were as blue as the gulf water when the sun breaks out after a storm. Donald felt more nervous than ever. But he knew he must make the most of his chance. He might not see Nancy alone again before Neil came. He caught her hand and stammered out,

" 'Nan, lass, I love you. You may think 'tis a hasty wooing, but that's a story I can tell you later maybe. I know well I'm not worthy of you, but if true love could make a man worthy there'd be none before me. Will you have me, Nan?'

"Nancy didn't *say* she would have him. She just *looked* it, and Donald kissed her right there in the snow.

"The next morning the storm was over. Donald knew Neil must be soon on his track. He did not want to make the Sherman house the scene of a quarrel, so he resolved to get away before the Campbell came. He persuaded Nancy to go with him to visit some friends in another settlement. As he brought Neil's sleigh up to the door he saw a black speck far out on the bay and laughed.

" 'Black Dan goes well, but he'll not be quick enough,' he said.

"Half an hour later Neil Campbell rushed into the Sherman kitchen and oh, how angry he was! There was nobody there but Betty Sherman, and Betty was not afraid of him. She was never afraid of anybody. She was very handsome, with hair as brown as October nuts and black eyes and crimson cheeks; and she had always been in love with Neil Campbell herself.

" 'Good morning, Mr. Campbell,' she said, with a toss of her head. 'It's early abroad you are. And on Black Dan, no less! Was I mistaken in thinking that Donald Fraser said once that his favourite horse should never be backed by any man but him? But doubtless a fair exchange is no robbery, and Brown Bess is a good mare in her way.'

" 'Where is Donald Fraser?' said Neil, shaking his fist. 'It's him I'm seeking, and it's him I will be finding. Where is he, Betty Sherman?'

" 'Donald Fraser is far enough away by this time,' mocked Betty. 'He is a prudent fellow, and has some quickness of wit under that sandy thatch of his. He came here last night at sunset, with a horse and sleigh not his own, or lately gotten, and he asked Nan in the stable yard to marry him. Did a man ask *me* to marry him at the cow's side, with a milking pail in my hand, it's a cold answer he'd get for his pains. But Nan thought differently, and they sat late together last night, and 'twas a bonny story Nan wakened me to hear when she came to bed—the story of a braw lover who let his secret out when the whisky was above the wit, and then fell asleep while his rival was away to woo and win his lass. Did you ever hear a like story, Mr. Campbell?'

" 'Oh, yes,' said Neil fiercely. 'It is laughing at me over the country side and telling that story that Donald Fraser will be doing, is it? But when I meet him it is not laughing he will be doing. Oh, no. There will be another story to tell!'

" 'Now, don't meddle with the man,' cried Betty. 'What a state to be in because one good-looking lass likes sandy hair and gray eyes better than Highland black and blue! You have not the spirit of a wren, Neil Campbell. Were I you, I would show Donald Fraser that I could woo and win a lass as speedily as any Lowlander of them all; that I would! There's many a girl would gladly say "yes" for your asking. And here stands one! Why not marry *me*, Neil Campbell? Folks say I'm as bonny as Nan—and I could love you as well as Nan loves her Donald—ay, and ten times better!'

"What do you suppose the Campbell did? Why, just the thing he ought to have done. He took Betty at her word on the spot; and there was a double wedding soon after. And it is said that Neil and Betty were the happiest couple in the world—happier even than Donald and Nancy. So all was well because it ended well!"

The Story Girl curtsied until her silken skirts swept the floor. Then she flung herself in her chair and looked at Mr. Campbell, flushed, triumphant, daring.

The story was old to us. It had once been published in a Charlottetown paper, and we had read in Aunt Olivia's scrapbook, where the Story Girl had learned it. But we had listened entranced. I have written down the bare words of the story, as she told it; but I can never reproduce the charm and colour and spirit she infused into it. It *lived* for us. Donald and Neil, Nancy and Betty, were there in that room with us. We saw the flashes of expression on their faces, we heard their voices, angry or tender, mocking or merry, in Lowland and Highland accent. We realized all the mingled coquetry and feeling and defiance and archness in Betty Sherman's daring speech. We had even forgotten all about Mr. Campbell.

That gentlemen, in silence, took out his wallet, extracted a note therefrom, and handed it gravely to the Story Girl.

"There are five dollars for you," he said, "and your story was well worth it. You *are* a wonder. Some day you will make the world realize it. I've been about a bit, and heard some good things, but I've never enjoyed anything more than that threadbare old story I heard in my cradle. And now, will you do me a favour?"

"Of course," said the delighted Story Girl.

"Recite the multiplication table for me," said Mr. Campbell.

We stared. Well might Mr. Campbell be called eccentric. What on earth did he want the multiplication table recited for? Even the Story Girl was surprised. But she began promptly, with twice one and went through it to twelve times twelve. She repeated it simply, but her voice changed from one tone to another as each in succession grew tired. We had never dreamed that there was so much in the multiplication table. As she announced it, the fact that three times three was nine was exquisitely ridiculous, five times six almost brought tears to our eyes, eight times seven was the most tragic and frightful thing ever heard of, and twelve times twelve rang like a trumpet call to victory.

Mr. Campbell nodded his satisfaction.

"I thought you could do it," he said. "The other day I found this statement in a book. 'Her voice would have made the multiplication table charming!' I thought of it when I heard yours. I didn't believe it before, but I do now."

Then he let us go.

"You see," said the Story Girl as we went home, "you need never be afraid of people."

"But we are not all Story Girls," said Cecily.

That night we heard Felicity talking to Cecily in their room.

"Mr. Campbell never noticed one of us except the Story Girl," she said, "but if *I* had put on *my* best dress as she did maybe she wouldn't have taken all the attention."

Could you ever do what Betty Sherman did, do you suppose?" asked Cecily absently.

"No; but I believe the Story Girl could," answered Felicity rather snappishly.

# CHAPTER VIII

# A
# *Tragedy
of Childhood*

THE Story Girl went to Charlottetown for a week in June to
visit Aunt Louisa. Life seemed very colourless without her, and
even Felicity admitted that it was lonesome. But three days after
her departure Felix told us something on the way home from
school which lent some spice to existence immediately.

"What do you think?" he said in a very solemn, yet excited,
tone. "Jerry Cowan told me at recess this afternoon that *he had
seen a picture of God*—that he has it at home in an old,
red-covered history of the world, and has looked at it *often*."

To think that Jerry Cowan should have seen such a picture
often! We were as deeply impressed as Felix had meant us to be.

"Did he say what it was like?" asked Peter.

"No—only that it was a picture of God, walking in the
garden of Eden."

"Oh," whispered Felicity—we all spoke in low tones on the
subject, for, by instinct and training, we thought and uttered
the Great Name with reverence, in spite of our devouring
curiosity—"oh, *would* Jerry Cowan bring it to school and let us
see it?"

"I asked him that, soon as ever he told me," said Felix. "He
said he might, but he couldn't promise, for he'd have to ask his
mother if he could bring the book to school. If she'll let him
he'll bring it to-morrow."

"Oh, I'll be almost afraid to look at it," said Sara Ray
tremulously.

I think we all shared her fear to some extent. Nevertheless,
we went to school the next day burning with curiosity. And we
were disappointed. Possibly night had brought counsel to Jerry
Cowan; or perhaps his mother had put him up to it. At all
events, he announced to us that he couldn't bring the red-

covered history to school, but if we wanted to buy the picture outright he would tear it out of the book and sell it to us for fifty cents.

We talked the matter over in serious conclave in the orchard that evening. We were all rather short of hard cash, having devoted most of our spare means to the school library fund. But the general consensus of opinion was that we must have the picture, no matter what pecuniary sacrifices were involved. If we could each give about seven cents we would have the amount. Peter could give only four, but Dan gave eleven, which squared matters.

"Fifty cents would be pretty dear for any other picture, but of course this is different," said Dan.

"And there's a picture of Eden thrown in, too, you know," added Felicity.

"Fancy selling God's picture," said Cecily in a shocked, awed tone.

"Nobody but a Cowan would do it, and that's a fact," said Dan.

"When we get it we'll keep it in the family Bible," said Felicity. "That's the only proper place."

"Oh, I wonder what it will be like," breathed Cecily.

We all wondered. Next day in school we agreed to Jerry Cowan's terms, and Jerry promised to bring the picture up to Uncle Alec's the following afternoon.

We were all intensely excited Saturday morning. To our dismay, it began to rain just before dinner.

"What if Jerry doesn't bring the picture to-day because of the rain?" I suggested.

"Never you fear," answered Felicity decidedly. "A Cowan would come through *anything* for fifty cents."

After dinner we all, without any verbal decision about it, washed our faces and combed our hair. The girls put on their second best dresses, and we boys donned white collars. We all had the unuttered feeling that we must do such honour to that Picture as we could. Felicity and Dan began a small spat over something, but stopped at once when Cecily said severely,

"How *dare* you quarrel when you are going to look at a picture of God to-day?"

Owing to the rain we could not foregather in the orchard, where we had meant to transact the business with Jerry. We did not wish our grown-ups around at our great moment, so we betook ourselves to the loft of the granary in the spruce wood, from whose window we could see the main road and hail Jerry. Sara Ray had joined us, very pale and nervous, having had, so it appeared, a difference of opinion with her mother about coming up the hill in the rain.

"I'm afraid I did very wrong to come against ma's will," she said miserably, "but I *couldn't* wait. I wanted to see the picture as soon as you did."

We waited and watched at the window. The valley was full of mist, and the rain was coming down in slanting lines over the tops of the spruces. But as we waited the clouds broke away and the sun came out flashingly; the drops on the spruce boughs glittered like diamonds.

"I don't believe Jerry can be coming," said Cecily in despair. "I suppose his mother must have thought it was dreadful, after all, to sell such a picture."

"There he is now!" cried Dan, waving excitedly from the window.

"He's carrying a fish-basket," said Felicity. "You surely don't suppose he would bring *that* picture in a fish-basket!"

Jerry *had* brought it in a fish-basket, as appeared when he mounted the granary stairs shortly afterwards. It was folded up in a newspaper packet on top of the dried herring with which the basket was filled. We paid him his money, but we would not open the packet until he had gone.

"Cecily," said Felicity in a hushed tone. "You are the best of us all. *You* open the parcel."

"Oh, I'm no gooder than the rest of you," breathed Cecily, "but I'll open it if you like."

With trembling fingers Cecily opened the parcel. We stood around, hardly breathing. She unfolded it and held it up. We saw it.

Suddenly Sara began to cry.

"Oh, oh, oh, does God look like *that*?" she wailed.

Felix and I spoke not. Disappointment, and something worse, sealed our speech. *Did* God look like that—like that stern, angrily-frowning old man with the tossing hair and beard of the wood-cut Cecily held.

"I suppose He must, since that is His picture," said Dan miserably.

"He looks awful cross," said Peter simply.

"Oh, I wish we'd never, never seen it," cried Cecily.

We all wished that—too late. Our curiosity had led us into some Holy of Holies, not to be profaned by human eyes, and this was our punishment.

"I've always had a feeling right along," wept Sara, "that it wasn't *right* to buy—or *look at*—God's picture."

As we stood there wretchedly we heard flying feet below and a blithe voice calling,

"Where are you, children?"

The Story Girl had returned! At any other moment we would have rushed to meet her in wild joy. But now we were too crushed and miserable to move.

"Whatever is the matter with you all?" demanded the Story Girl, appearing at the top of the stairs. "What is Sara crying about? What have you got there?"

"A picture of God," said Cecily with a sob in her voice, "and oh, it is so dreadful and ugly. Look!"

The Story Girl looked. An expression of scorn came over her face.

"Surely you don't believe God looks like that," she said impatiently, while her fine eyes flashed. "He doesn't—He couldn't. He is wonderful and beautiful. I'm surprised at you. *That* is nothing but the picture of a cross old man."

Hope sprang up in our hearts, although we were not wholly convinced.

"I don't know," said Dan dubiously. "It says under the picture 'God in the Garden of Eden.' It's *printed*."

"Well, I suppose that's what the man who drew it thought God was like," answered the Story Girl carelessly. "But *he* couldn't have known any more than you do. *He* had never seen Him."

"It's all very well for you to say so," said Felicity, "but *you* don't know either. I wish I could believe that isn't like God—but I don't know what to believe."

"Well, if you won't believe me, I suppose you'll believe the minister," said the Story Girl. "Go and ask him. He's in the house this very minute. He came up with us in the buggy."

At any other time we would never have dared catechize the minister about anything. But desperate cases call for desperate measures. We drew straws to see who should go and do the asking, and the lot fell to Felix.

"Better wait until Mr. Marwood leaves, and catch him in the lane," advised the Story Girl. "You'll have a lot of grown-ups around you in the house."

Felix took her advice. Mr. Marwood, presently walking benignantly along the lane, was confronted by a fat, small boy with a pale face but resolute eyes.

The rest of us remained in the background but within hearing.

"Well, Felix, what is it?" asked Mr. Marwood kindly.

"Please, sir, does God really look like this?" asked Felix, holding out the picture. "We hope He doesn't—but we want to know the truth, and that is why I'm bothering you. Please excuse us and tell me."

The minister looked at the picture. A stern expression came into his gentle blue eyes and he got as near to frowning as it was possible for him to get.

"Where did you get that thing?" he asked.

*Thing!* We began to breath easier.

"We bought it from Jerry Cowan. He found it in a red-covered history of the world. It *says* it's God's picture," said Felix.

"It is nothing of the sort," said Mr. Marwood indignantly. "There is no such thing as a picture of God, Felix. No human being knows what He looks like—no human being *can* know. We should not even try to think what He looks like. But, Felix, you may be sure that God is infinitely more beautiful and loving and tender and kind than anything we can imagine of Him. Never believe anything else, my boy. As for this—this *sacrilege*—take it and burn it."

We did not know what a sacrilege meant, but we knew that Mr. Marwood had declared that the picture was not like God. That was enough for us. We felt as if a terrible weight had been lifted from our minds.

"I could hardly believe the Story Girl, but of course the minister *knows*," said Dan happily.

"We've lost fifty cents because of it," said Felicity gloomily.

We had lost something of infinitely more value than fifty cents, although we did not realize it just then. The minister's words had removed from our minds the bitter belief that God was like that picture; but on something deeper and more enduring than mind an impression had been made that was never to be removed. The mischief was done. From that day to this the thought or the mention of God brings up before us involuntarily the vision of a stern, angry, old man. Such was the price we were to pay for the indulgence of a curiosity which each of us, deep in our hearts, had, like Sara Ray, felt ought not to be gratified.

"Mr. Marwood told me to burn it," said Felix.

"It doesn't seem reverent to do that," said Cecily. "Even if it isn't God's picture, it has His name on it."

"Bury it," said the Story Girl.

We did bury it after tea, in the depths of the spruce grove; and then we went into the orchard. It was so nice to have the Story Girl back again. She had wreathed her hair with Canterbury Bells, and looked like the incarnation of rhyme and story and dream.

"Canterbury Bells is a lovely name for a flower, isn't it?" she said. "It makes you think of cathedrals and chimes, doesn't it? Let's go over to Uncle Stephen's Walk, and sit on the branches of the big tree. It's too wet on the grass, and I know a story—a *true* story, about an old lady I saw in town at Aunt Louisa's. Such a dear old lady, with lovely silvery curls."

After the rain the air seemed dripping with odours in the warm west wind—the tang of fir balsam, the spice of mint, the wild woodsiness of ferns, the aroma of grasses steeping in the sunshine,—and with it all a breath of wild sweetness from far hill pastures.

Scattered through the grass in Uncle Stephen's Walk, were blossoming pale, aerial flowers which had no name that we could ever discover. Nobody seemed to know anything about them. They had been there when Great-grandfather King bought the place. I have never seen them elsewhere, or found them described in any floral catalogue. We called them the White Ladies. The Story Girl gave them the name. She said they looked like the souls of good women who had had to suffer much and had been very patient. They were wonderfully dainty, with a strange, faint, aromatic perfume which was only to be detected at a little distance and vanished if you bent over them. They faded soon after they were plucked; and, although strangers, greatly admiring them, often carried away roots and seeds, they could never be coaxed to grow elsewhere.

"My story is about Mrs. Dunbar and the Captain of the *Fanny*," said the Story Girl, settling herself comfortably on a bough, with her brown head against a gnarled trunk. "It's sad and beautiful—and true. I do love to tell stories that I know really happened. Mrs. Dunbar lives next door to Aunt Louisa in town. She is so sweet. You wouldn't think to look at her that she had a tragedy in her life, but she has. Aunt Louisa told me the tale. It all happened long, long ago. Interesting things like this all did happen long ago, it seems to me. They never seem to happen now. This was in '49, when people were rushing to the gold fields in California. It was just like a fever, Aunt Louisa says. People took it, right here on the Island; and a number of young men determined they would go to California.

"It is easy to go to California now; but it was a very different matter then. There were no railroads across the land, as there are now, and if you wanted to go to California you had to go in a sailing vessel, all the way around Cape Horn. It was a long and dangerous journey; and sometimes it took over six months. When you got there you had no way of sending word home again except by the same plan. It might be over a year before your people at home heard a word about you—and fancy what their feelings would be!

"But these young men didn't think of these things; they were led on by a golden vision. They made all their arrangements, and they chartered the brig *Fanny* to take them to California.

"The captain of the *Fanny* is the hero of my story. His name was Alan Dunbar, and he was young and handsome. Heroes always are, you know, but Aunt Louisa says he really was. And he was in love—wildly in love,—with Margaret Grant. Margaret was as beautiful as a dream, with soft blue eyes and clouds of golden hair; and she loved Alan Dunbar just as much as he loved her. But her parents were bitterly opposed to him, and they had forbidden Margaret to see him or speak to him. They hadn't anything against him as a *man*, but they didn't want her to throw herself away on a sailor.

"Well, when Alan Dunbar knew that he must go to California in the *Fanny* he was in despair. He felt that he could *never* go so far away for so long and leave his Margaret behind. And

Margaret felt that she could never let him go. I know *exactly* how she felt."

"How can you know?" interrupted Peter suddenly. "You ain't old enough to have a beau. How can you know?"

The Story Girl looked at Peter with a frown. She did not like to be interrupted when telling a story.

"Those are not things one *knows* about," she said with dignity. "One *feels* about them."

Peter, crushed but not convinced, subsided, and the Story Girl went on.

"Finally, Margaret ran away with Alan, and they were married in Charlottetown. Alan intended to take his wife with him to California in the *Fanny*. If it was a hard journey for a man it was harder still for a woman, but Margaret would have dared anything for Alan's sake. They had three days—*only* three days—of happiness, and then the blow fell. The crew and the passengers of the *Fanny* refused to let Captain Dunbar take his wife with him. They told him he must leave her behind. And all his prayers were of no avail. They say he stood on the deck of the *Fanny* and pleaded with the men while the tears ran down his face; but they would not yield, and he had to leave Margaret behind. Oh, what a parting it was!"

There was heartbreak in the Story Girl's voice and tears came into our eyes. There, in the green bower of Uncle Stephen's Walk, we cried over the pathos of a parting whose anguish had been stilled for many years.

"When it was all over, Margaret's father and mother forgave her, and she went back home to wait—to *wait*. Oh, it is so dreadful just to *wait*, and do nothing else. Margaret waited for nearly a year. How long it must have seemed to her! And at last there came a letter—but not from Alan. Alan was *dead*. He had died in California and had been buried there. While Margaret had been thinking of him and longing for him and praying for him he had been lying in his lonely, faraway grave."

Cecily sprang up, shaking with sobs.

"Oh, don't—don't go on," she implored. "I *can't* bear any more."

"There is no more," said the Story Girl. "That was the end of it—the end of everything for Margaret. It didn't kill *her*, but her heart died."

"I just wish I'd hold of those fellows who wouldn't let the Captain take his wife," said Peter savagely.

"Well, it was awful sad," said Felicity, wiping her eyes. "But it was long ago and we can't do any good by crying over it now. Let us go and get something to eat. I made some nice little rhubarb tarts this morning."

We went. In spite of new disappointments and old heart-breaks we had appetites. And Felicity did make scrumptious rhubarb tarts!